BIRTHRIGHT

DOCTOR WHO – THE NEW ADVENTURES

Also available:

TIMEWYRM: GENESYS by John Peel
TIMEWYRM: EXODUS by Terrance Dicks
TIMEWYRM: APOCALYPSE by Nigel Robinson
TIMEWYRM: REVELATION by Paul Cornell

CAT'S CRADLE: TIME'S CRUCIBLE by Marc Platt
CAT'S CRADLE: WARHEAD by Andrew Cartmel
CAT'S CRADLE: WITCH MARK by Andrew Hunt

NIGHTSHADE by Mark Gatiss
LOVE AND WAR by Paul Cornell
TRANSIT by Ben Aaronovitch
THE HIGHEST SCIENCE by Gareth Roberts
THE PIT by Neil Penswick
DECEIT by Peter Darvill-Evans
LUCIFER RISING by Jim Mortimore and Andy Lane
WHITE DARKNESS by David McIntee
SHADOWMIND by Christopher Bulis

BIRTHRIGHT

Nigel Robinson

First published in Great Britain in 1993 by
Doctor Who Books
an imprint of Virgin Publishing Ltd
332 Ladbroke Grove
London W10 5AH

ISBN 0 426 20393 3

Cover illustration by Peter Elson

Typeset by Type Out, Mitcham CR4 2AG

Printed and bound in Great Britain by
Cox & Wyman Ltd, Reading, Berks

CONTENTS

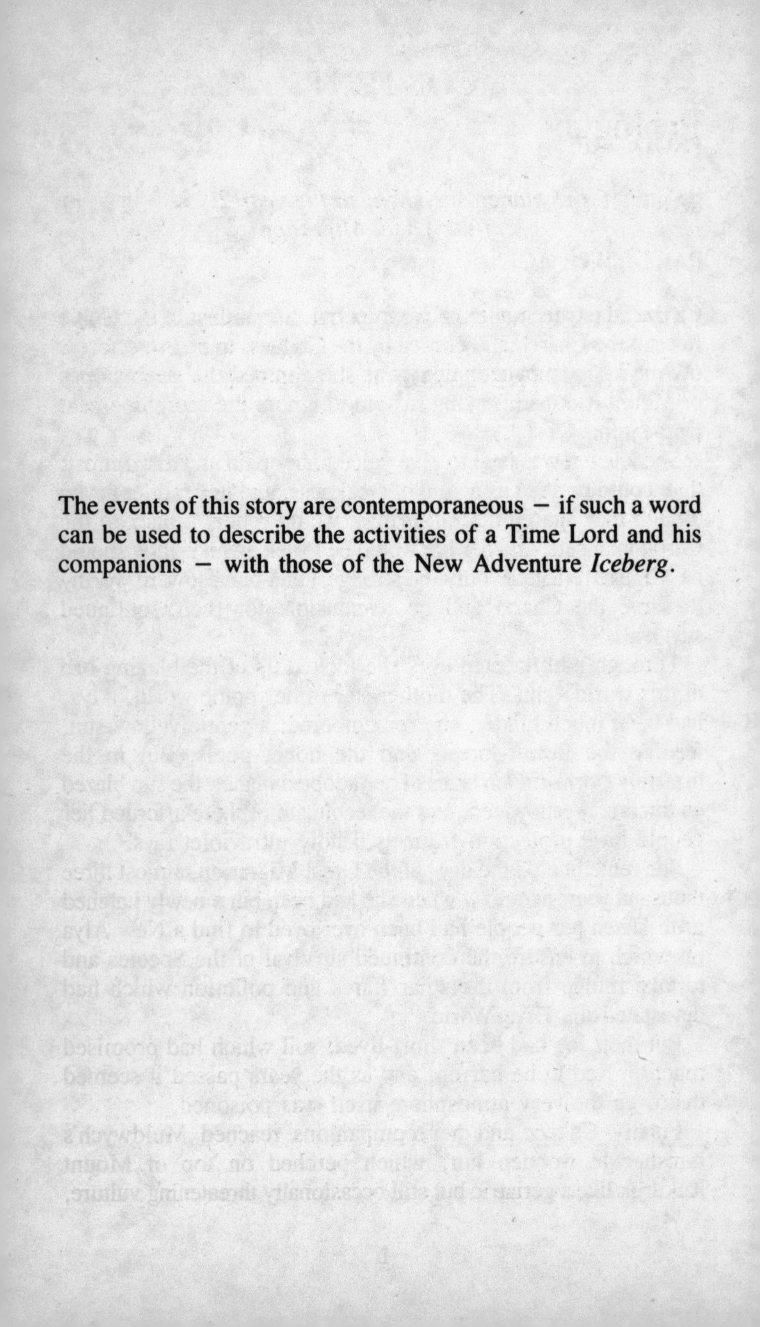

The events of this story are contemporaneous – if such a word can be used to describe the activities of a Time Lord and his companions – with those of the New Adventure *Iceberg*.

Prologue:

The planet Antýkhon, in the year 2,959
of the Great Migration

Ch'tizz, the Queen of the Hive Imperial, Stewardess of the Noble Race of the Charrl, and chosen by the Goddess to be Protectoress of Antýkhon, moaned silently as she climbed the steep slopes of Mount Kukūruk, trying in vain to ignore the scorching heat of the sun.

She knew it was fatal to give voice to her pain and discomfort: that would be seen as a sign of weakness, and her retinue, even though they shared her sufferings, would report it back to the Chronomancers, and her life would be forfeit. As it rightly should be, Ch'tizz reflected: only the strongest and bravest were worthy to serve the Charrl and be responsible for their continued survival.

Through multifaceted eyes she looked up at the blazing orb of this world's sun. The mother star of her home world, Alya, had been much kinder, she remembered: a gentle yellow sun, feeding the flower-forests and the honey-pools. But in the bizarrely storm-ridden skies of her adopted planet, the sun blazed an unnatural yellow-red, and the feeble atmosphere afforded her people little protection from its deadly ultraviolet rays.

She remembered the days of the Great Migration, almost three thousand years ago now, when she had been but a newly hatched grub. Then her people had been overjoyed to find a New Alya on which to ensure the continued survival of the Species and to take refuge from the solar flares and pollution which had devastated the Hive World.

But their joy had been short-lived: soil which had promised much proved to be barren, and as the years passed it seemed that even the very atmosphere itself was poisoned.

Finally Ch'tizz and her companions reached Muldwych's ramshackle wooden hut, which perched on top of Mount Kukūruk like a geriatric but still occasionally threatening vulture, watching over the vast and empty plains below. She indicated to her colleagues that they should wait outside, and then bent down to pass through the low doorway.

Muldwych glanced up from a huge, leather-bound book as Ch'tizz entered the room. His lined and ruddy face, which hadn't seen a razor or a bar of soap for several days, betrayed no surprise at the royal visitation; rather it was almost as if he had been expecting the Queen of the Hive. For a long time.

He put the book down, ran a hand through his untidy grey-brown hair, and eased himself to his feet, bowing as far as his rotund form would allow.

'Your Majesty, it's indeed a great honour,' he smiled. A little too smugly, thought Ch'tizz, but she let it pass.

She had never liked Muldwych, but she tolerated him because of the secrets he had revealed to her Elders and for the great and welcome services he often performed for the Hive Race. Besides, he was now the Charrl's only hope.

Muldwych offered her the threadbare easy chair in which he had been sitting, and Ch'tizz hesitated, casting a wary eye towards the door. Muldwych smiled again.

'It's perfectly all right, ma'am,' he said softly. 'Your courtiers dare not enter my hut. So, if you are tired, you may rest yourself here.'

He knows too much, thought Ch'tizz, but sat down nevertheless.

Her antennae, normally wrapped tightly around her bare, hard skull, quivered and expanded slightly, reacting with distaste to the sickly-sweet Mammal-stench emanating from the human.

Ch'tizz tried to ignore the cloying smell which made others of her race physically sick; after all, it was widely said that the Mammals found the body odours of the Charrl just as pungent and revolting.

'Muldwych, you have done much for my people over the years,' Ch'tizz began in her thin rasping voice, which nevertheless carried a true sense of power.

'You know that has been a privilege, my dear lady,' said Muldwych, pulling out a small wooden stool and squatting down at the Queen's right hand. He took a pipe from out of the pocket of his waistcoat. 'May I?'

'Of course,' said Ch'tizz, 'though what pleasure you can gain from such a habit confounds me.'

Muldwych grinned, and puffed away on the pipe. 'An old man alone on his mountain must have his pleasures,' he chuckled. 'Now, how may I help you?'

'The Charrl are dying, Muldwych,' said Ch'tizz. 'Our seed is thin, and the planet we chose as the New Alya we have discovered to be a dead and forgotten world.'

Muldwych looked slightly put out, but said: 'Dying, but not yet dead, your Majesty. Although it's not in the best of health, I'll allow that.'

'The best of health?' said the Queen. 'I tell you, Muldwych, it's dead! We must purify every drop of water before we can drink from a stream. Our grubs and pupae are dying because there is not enough meat, or oxygen in the air to support them, nor enough nutrients in the soil to feed them. Another thousand years on this planet and we will all be extinct!'

'Which shows a lack of judgement on the part of your Philosophers and Chronomancers when they chose Antýkhon as a colony world,' Muldwych remarked.

Ch'tizz ignored the slight, which, within the Hive itself, would have sent the speaker into instant exile.

'Our Philosophers decided that at one time this planet was capable of supporting the most varied forms of Life in all known Existence.'

Muldwych nodded. 'True enough. Most planets can bear no more than several thousand thousand species to preserve its ecosystems and food chains. Antýkhon, on the other hand, and if my research into the fossils here is correct, once teemed with millions upon uncountable millions of different life forms. Curious, that.'

'And now it can hardly bear the few native species which have stubbornly remained on it.'

'In which case, surely your Hives should start organizing another Migration to a more suitable and fertile world?'

'You know as well as I do, Muldwych, that our resources are exhausted,' rasped Ch'tizz, rapidly losing her patience. 'We no longer have the minerals to power the engines of our gravity-ships, which lie disused and forgotten in the spaceports of this world. And, even if we did, do you realize the number of planets there are in this Sector which could support the Charrl? Our Philosophers say there is not one suitable planet within a radius of ten thousand parsecs. Our race is weakened: it could never survive the centuries another Migration would require.'

Muldwych puffed thoughtfully on his pipe, filling the small hut with thick blue clouds of smoke.

'All life must sometime come to an end,' he said philosophically. 'Everything gets old and falls apart in time; it even happens to me . . . '

Ch'tizz leapt up from the chair, her powerful hindlegs shaking and rattling with emotion, and drew herself up to her full height of over seven feet. '*But not the Charrl!*' she cried.

For a few long seconds the Charrl Queen and the Mammal stared at each other, the one defiantly refusing to betray any emotion to the other.

Then Muldwych smiled, and stood up to walk over to a stove in the corner of the hut on which a cast-iron pan of water was boiling merrily. Silently, he poured the water into an earthenware mug.

A heady aroma arose from the mug. He sipped at his drink, gazing at Ch'tizz over the rim of the mug, deliberately prolonging the silence.

'Tea,' he explained to Ch'tizz's unspoken question. 'A noxious infusion of dried leaves . . . '

Ch'tizz said nothing, just stared through unblinking eyes at Muldwych. The mandibles in her mighty jaw clenched and unclenched with both anticipation and impatience, and gobs of acidic saliva dripped down onto the rush-covered floor.

He knows what we are asking, she thought. *Must he prolong our agony?*

Muldwych took another long slurp of his tea, and looked thoughtfully at the Queen over the rim of his mug. Finally he spoke.

'The Charrl, the noblest species this galaxy has ever known. The race of the greatest poets and the finest philosophers,' he reflected. 'The race of the faithfulest friends, creators, so they say, of over three hundred of the six hundred and ninety-nine Wonders of the Universe. Never once in over five thousand years did they go to war with another race except in self-defence. The Charrl, the mightiest Venerators of Life this Universe has ever known –'

'It is the will of the Goddess,' Ch'tizz interrupted. 'All Life is sacred and must be revered – you of all people should know that.'

'I do. And it is because of your Reverence For All Things that it has been my pleasure to help you in the past. And now you want my help again. But why?' asked Muldwych, although he already knew the answer.

'We need a new Hive,' said Ch'tizz simply.

'But you said that your race could not survive another Migration to a new star,' said Muldwych.

The accursed Mammal is enjoying this, thought Ch'tizz furiously. But when she replied her voice was steady and even.

'It cannot. But there are – other ways. We lack physical strength, or the technology to build new gravity-ships; but we still have the power of our minds.'

'Indeed, a race with greater psychic powers I've never heard of . . . '

'We must act now, while we still live. You are a man of great intelligence and experience, Muldwych –'

'I've some book-learning,' he said modestly, and gestured at the packed and creaking shelves behind him. 'All theory, of course,' he lied. 'Then I've met some interesting characters in my life who've shared the odd secret with me . . . '

'There are few indigenous specimens left on this planet,' continued Ch'tizz. 'But, of them all, our Philosophers say that you are the wisest, the most powerful –'

'I assure you that I am but –'

'*The most powerful,*' Ch'tizz repeated firmly. 'They say that you even possess the knowledge to call back yesterday, to turn on its head the very flow of time itself.'

'It's the result of living alone on Mount Kukūruk with only the daisies for company,' he said flippantly. 'It makes an old man believe any amount of foolish things.'

'No.'

Muldwych looked at the Queen through narrowed, distrusting eyes.

Now I have him, the Mammal, thought Ch'tizz. *Now he knows who is in command here!*

Muldwych put down his mug and went to the small window, and peered through the plexiglass screen which protected him from the elements. He looked thoughtfully into the distance, and, with a strange sadness, down at the great plain below, shrouded in what seemed an eternal night.

Long ago he had been witness to the killing of the last survivor of a noble and graceful species down on that plain. Must the Charrl go the same way?

Finally he turned decisively back to Ch'tizz.

'So. What would you like me to do?'

Long hours later Ch'tizz left Muldwych's hut on Mount Kukū-ruk and returned with her retinue to the Hive Imperial, some four thousand miles away. It was a hard journey, across an entire sun-scorched continent, and several dangerous seas, and many of her court were lost on the trip. But, if the physiognomy of the Charrl had allowed her the facial muscles to do so, Ch'tizz would have smiled all the way.

Muldwych had agreed to the audacious plan, for which he would be justly rewarded. But most importantly of all the future of the noble race of the Charrl was assured.

Muldwych had promised that; and, though his plan might take almost five hundred years, it was well known that Muldwych, like the Charrl themselves, always kept his promises.

Ch'tizz granted herself the indulgence of a small ironic laugh. The *future* of the Charrl! If only her people knew!

Left alone, once more, in his hut on Mount Kukūruk, Muldwych smiled a self-satisfied smile and rubbed his hands with glee, scarcely able to contain his joy.

He had convinced the Queen that she was in charge, that he was following *her* orders and not the other way round. He was really most extraordinarily good at manipulating people, he thought. At long last his carefully laid scheme was coming to fruition; and, if it helped the Charrl also, then all well and good.

He drained the last of his tea and burped. He shook his head: he really shouldn't put that much whisky in his tea, he thought.

At his age he ought to know better, especially when he had at least another five hundred years to wait . . .

Interlude

Ercildoune, Scotland, AD 1270

The young stable hand Tommy had no idea why his lord and master had asked him to ride through the glen on this dark and foggy morning, in order to be at the nearby market town by first light. He had a casket of French wine to be picked up, he'd said; but hadn't the strange wee man, in whose service Tommy had been for two years now, taken receipt of another consignment only the day before yesterday?

Still, he knew better than to question his master's mysterious ways, even when it meant leaving the bed of the lovely Annie McLaren, the new flame-haired serving girl. Tommy would do anything for his lord, even though he would be the first to admit that he was a weird one.

Hardly ever at his ancestral hall, when he did return from his trips to other lands, he remained for most of the time in his rooms, poring over old manuscripts, or talking softly to himself in a sing-song language that the young stable lad couldn't recognize.

'You've been a good lad to me, Tommy,' he had said with a strange note of finality, when he bade him farewell some hours ago.

And even that was odd: usually his lord was asleep until dawn, but this morning he had got up especially early to see him off. As though he was checking that everything was going to plan.

'Ride carefully now,' he had said to him, while patting Old Dory, the mare who was pulling the cart. Then he had added cryptically: 'And should anyone give you the choice, take the bonny, bonny road . . . '

But he was a good man, of that the stable lad had no doubt. He had taken him in when all around him, even his family, had disowned him on account of the mysterious and near-debilitating wasting sickness he had.

No, not just a good man, he reflected, but a wise and caring man as well. He had prescribed potions to ward off the more unpleasant effects of the illness, and make his final years at least bearable.

There were gossips in the town who said that he tended to the care of King Alexander as well, and that he had even once been summoned to England by the great Edward Plantagenet himself! Whether those stories were true or not, the young stable lad knew that he loved his lord and master dearly and that, like many others who had been and would be taken into his master's circle, he would trust him with his life.

Old Dory stopped in her tracks and the stable hand gave her a whip on the rump to urge her on. Instead she neighed obstinately and refused to move.

Tommy frowned. Old Dory might be approaching the end of her days (which makes two of us, he thought sadly), but she'd always been a reliable mare. Why wasn't she going further?

The stable hand jumped off the cart and peered into the early-morning mist: he could see the tall stately figure of a fine lady approaching him.

What was she doing about so early in the morning? Didn't she know it was dangerous for a well-born lady to be walking alone by herself? His nose twitched as he detected a pungent odour coming from the lady's direction; the astringent smell began to make his eyes water.

'Hello. Who are you?' he asked in his native Gaelic.

'I have come for thee, Thomas,' she said, and reached out a long, elegant, but strangely skeletal hand to him.

As he touched her Tommy felt a thrill of wellbeing course through his veins, and his limbs seemed to gain a new-found vigour. He looked up at the fine lady's face, but it was shrouded in mist.

The tall lady looked down fondly – surely not lustfully? – at the young stable lad.

'We must make a pact together, you and I,' she said.

True Thomas lay on Huntlie bank;
A ferlie he spied wi' his e'e;
And there he saw a ladye bright
Come riding down by the Eildon Tree . . .

'Now ye maun go wi' me,' she said,
'True Thomas, ye maun go wi' me;
And ye maun serve me many years,
Thro' weal or woe as may chance to be.'

– *Traditional Ballad*

Letter to The Times *from Katharine Stephen of Godmanchester*
Thursday 2 July 1908

It was in the north-east and of a bright flame-colour like the light of sunrise or sunset. The sky for some distance above the light which appeared to be in the horizon, was blue as in the daytime, with bands of light cloud of a pinkish colour at intervals. Only the brightest stars could be seen in any part of the sky, although it was an almost cloudless night. It was possible to read large print indoors, and the hands of the clock were quite distinct. I have never at any time seen anything the least like this in England, and it would be most interesting if anyone would explain the cause of so unusual a sight.

Part One

BENNY

The planet Earth, AD 1289 – AD 1909

[illegible] then [illegible] and a face [illegible] the [illegible] housekeeping [illegible] change [illegible] after him [illegible] his hiccups [illegible] the revellers in the [illegible] the sounds and songs of [illegible] sound of the clattering [illegible] for the start of early [illegible]

[illegible] heart is a [illegible] of the East End that [illegible] most com- [illegible] the world had ever

Chapter 1

London, 2.30 a.m., Wednesday 3 February AD 1909

Outside the Ten Bells pub in London's Commercial Street Ernie Wright was in a good mood. All right, so he might have drunk more than might be good for him, and the wife and three kids would have a fit when he arrived home stinking of cheap tobacco, and even cheaper booze. They'd be even more put out when they discovered that he'd already spent tonight more than half the weekly wage he earned as a butcher down at Smithfield meat market.

But Ernie didn't care. Not when at his right hand, helping him to stand upright and maintain some semblance of sobriety, was Lancashire Lily, who Ernie had decided was probably the most beautiful girl in the world.

Well, in Spitalfields at least. All right, so she might have too much paint on her face, and maybe at seventeen she was a little young, but then that was the way Ernie liked them.

Not that he *had* to pay for it, you understand. No, even in his early forties, with a belly bloated with beer and a face ruddied with cheap gin, Ernie Wright could still charm the ladies. But if Lily needed a few shillings for the housekeeping then Ernie, gent that he was, would be only too happy to oblige.

Lancashire Lily looked up at Ernie fondly as she steadied him, and patted him on the back in an attempt to stop his hiccups. Behind them they could hear the noise of the revellers in the pub, while down the road there came the shouts and songs of the traders at Spitalfields market and the sound of the clattering as they began unloading their wagons ready for the start of early-morning trading.

It was a sound which warmed Ernie's drunken heart: a comforting reassurance from the heart of the East End that England was still the centre of the hardest-working, most commercially successful business operation the world had ever known. Yes, decided Ernie, the East End is alive with good and honest toil, King Edward the Seventh's on his throne, and all was well with the Empire and the world. And I'm walking down the road with Lancashire Lily!

'What time's it, Lily?' he asked, slurring his words.

Lily pointed down to the elaborate pocket-watch on Ernie's waistcoat: she'd had her eye on it all evening.

'Half past two in the morning, dearie,' she said in her Prestonian accent, mentally kicking herself for forgetting the name of her companion. 'Time you was getting back to the missus.'

'But not before first escorting such a lovely lady safely home,' he declared drunkenly.

'Well . . . if you insist,' Lily said with practised coyness. 'I've got a couple of rooms just a little way down there in Fournier Street . . . '

' 'S my pleashure, Lily,' Ernie said effusively. 'After all, 's a foggy night and a lady can't be too careful these daysh, cansshe?'

'What d'you mean?'

'Well, there's many a villain about in these violent timesh,' Ernie whispered. 'The Ripper, for instance . . . '

Lily giggled nervously.

'Old Jack?' she asked. 'He's been dead these twenty years or more now. No, there's nowt to fear from him. 'Less his ghost comes back to haunt us, that is! You don't believe in ghosts, do you?'

'Who, me?' asked Ernie, trying to suppress a burp. 'Course not.'

'That's just as well,' said Lily as she took his arm and steered him down the street. 'They do say there's been some right peculiar happenings round here lately though.'

Ernie turned around at her, interested, and then became even more interested as he saw Lily's ample bosoms heaving beneath her threadbare coat.

'There's them that say there's been some strange ap-par-it-ions,' she said, pronouncing the unfamiliar word with care. 'Why, only yesterday Mollie Wilkins told me she'd seen a big brute of a man hiding in the shadows. But when she went up to him – to see what his business was, you understand – there was nothing to be seen. Like he'd vanished in smoke.'

By this time they had turned off the main road, and the cries of the porters at Spitalfields market had faded to a distant hum. Here in the back streets of Whitechapel, away from the street lamps and the light of the cloud-covered moon, the fog seemed even thicker, cutting into Ernie's throat like a rusty old knife.

The butcher shuddered and pulled his coat tighter around himself: it might be February but it was still bitterly cold and all this talk of ghosts had made him even chillier.

Lily noticed his discomfort, and patted his arm reassuringly.

'Now, don't you go and worry yourself, dearie,' she said soothingly. 'I live just at the bottom of this street on the corner. I'll warm you up with a nice cuppa Rosie –' she winked suggestively – 'and who knows what else, eh?'

Ernie grinned, and tried to steal a drunken kiss from Lily, who pushed him off playfully.

'Now, don't you come all over like that,' she said teasingly. 'Least not till we're inside.' She coughed. 'By heck, what's that ruddy smell – it's not you, is it?'

'What smell?' asked Ernie, suddenly trying to remember the last time he had had a bath.

'Dunno,' said Lily and coughed again. 'It's bitter, sharp – like, like smelling salts . . . ' She shrugged. 'Well, whatever it is, it can wait.'

She dug into her coat pockets for the key to her front door. Suddenly she felt Ernie's body stiffen and tense. She looked up.

'What's the –'

The punter had come from out of nowhere. One second there was nothing in front of Ernie and Lily and the next the tall figure was standing between them and the front door. Lily jumped back, startled, but she was a hardened girl of the streets and quickly regained her composure.

'Crikey, you didn't half give me a shock there, guv,' she said, and screwed up her nose. The acrid smell of ammonia was even stronger now: it hung about the stranger like a cloud, and its pungency made Lily's eyes water.

'Now, come on, luvvie, let me pass,' said Lily sternly.

The stranger made no sound. By Lily's side, Ernie was getting worried: this was not another drunk looking for a good time before going home to the wife: this was something *different*.

Lily, however, was getting annoyed. She was about to give the stranger a well-deserved piece of her mind when the moon came out from behind the clouds, and washed the alleyway in its blue unearthly light.

Through large bulbous eyes the stranger glanced sharply up at the moon, and hissed, its identity now revealed.

Ernie gasped in terror at the stranger's appearance, but Lily didn't even have time to scream. She was suddenly aware of a sharp crisp pain, ripping from her groin up to her breasts. She clutched at her stomach, and frowned as she found it sticky and warm with blood.

Another lightning-quick slash from the stranger's arm and with a horrified detachment Lily felt her bladder and guts tumble, steaming and hot, from out of her belly, and onto the ground.

'Ernie . . . ' she gasped, finally remembering his name, and slammed lifeless to the cobblestoned ground.

The stranger whipped out a long skeletal arm at the terrified and white-faced Ernie. Suddenly sober, he leapt back and turned and staggered back down the alleyway.

The creature in the shadows snarled and pulled back onto its haunches, debating for a second whether to follow Ernie.

No, he was not the one it was interested in, and time was already running short. Through unfeeling and lidless eyes, the creature in the fog stared down detachedly at Lily's bloodied and steaming carcase, and, with practised and studied skill, began cutting up her corpse.

Ernie didn't stop running until he reached Spitalfields market, where many of the porters and traders knew him from long drinking sessions in the Ten Bells and surrounding pubs. Finally reaching the safety of the market, Ernie flung himself down onto the ground, at the same time upsetting a cart of fruit.

'What the flamin' – ' began the disgruntled costermonger until he saw Ernie's ashen face and his chattering teeth.

'Who is it?' came one voice.

'It's old Ernie Wright – what's he about?'

'If I know Ernie he's had one too many!'

'Four or five too many, if you ask me!'

'Nah, look at him – he's sober – as sober as a judge . . . '

By now a crowd had gathered round the terrified Ernie who, unable to give voice to his fears, could only point in the general direction of Fournier Street. Several of the tradesmen looked nervously at each other: twenty years on, the threat of the Ripper was still firm in their minds.

'What's going on here?' asked an authoritative voice, and the traders looked up to see the figure of young Constable Reggie Hawkins, the local bobby, slightly the worse for wear after a couple of gins down at another of the local pubs.

'It's Ernie, Reggie! Come and 'ave a look!'

Hawkins bent down to look at the ashen face of the neighbourhood meat trader. 'C'mon, now, Ernie,' he said gently. 'What is it?'

Ernie continued to point in the direction of Fournier Street. His lips trembled, but finally he found his voice: 'L-l-Lily . . . '

'Now who's Lily, Ernie?' asked Hawkins.

'Fournier Street . . . '

'Lil Nuttall, he means,' volunteered one of the porters. 'They call her Lancashire Lily round here.'

'Ah yes . . . ' said Hawkins, slightly embarrassed. He'd more than once availed himself of Lily's services, in return for turning a blind eye to her law-breaking.

'She's been murdered!' Ernie said.

Suddenly sober, Hawkins took Ernie by the arm and ran off in the direction of Fournier Street, with a large crowd of porters and market traders on their heels.

When he saw Lily's butchered body the constable felt the bile rising in his throat; it was all he could do not to throw up. As it was, he found himself trembling uncontrollably.

Lily's body had been totally gutted, and through the gaping hole in her front Hawkins could see her the bare bones of her rib cage. By Lily's body her guts, still red and steaming in the cold night air, had been laid in a neat pile. Of the murderer there was no sign.

'Who did this, Ernie?' demanded Hawkins.

'S-S-S –'

'Speak up, man!'

Ernie took a deep breath, and attempted to give Hawkins a description of the man he had only seen in the supernatural light of the moon: the bulbous eyes, set in a grinning death's head of a face; the gangly limbs.

'I tell you, Reggie, he were like a bloomin' great grasshopper, that's what he was.'

'Springheel Jack!' gasped one of the women who had come to look at the body. 'He's come back!'

'Don't be daft!' retorted Hawkins. 'Springheel Jack's a legend!' Hawkins had just been moved to this beat: the last thing he wanted was for his patch to get a reputation for being haunted.

'She's right,' said another woman in the crowd. 'The little imp terrorized us last century, and we never caught him. My bet is he's come back to get his revenge.'

By now quite a crowd had gathered, all eager to catch a glimpse of the corpse. Many of them had been living in the area at the time of the Ripper murders and couldn't believe their luck to be in at the beginning of what could be the start of another similar series of murders.

'She's been butchered . . . ' said one.

'Yeah, *butchered* . . . ' said another.

Suddenly all eyes were turned on Ernie.

Ernie was frozen to the spot, as Constable Hawkins took his arm again, this time a little too forcefully for comfort.

'That's right,' he said. 'Butchered. And you're a butcher now, aren't you, Ernie? Just what were you doing with this girl then?'

'We were just having a bit of fun, that's all,' Ernie insisted nervously. 'You don't think I did it, did you?'

'You are a butcher, aren't you, Ernie?' he repeated.

'Leave him alone,' came a soft but firm voice from the crowd.

Constable Hawkins turned around, and peered at the stranger. He was small and short-haired, dressed uncomfortably in an opera cloak and wing-collar shirt, and leaning on an elaborately carved walking-cane. Another nob out for the night and slumming it, the policeman thought.

'What did you say, guv?'

'Leave him alone,' the stranger repeated. 'He didn't do it.'

'Oh?' said Hawkins, and peered at the other man, whose face was hidden in the shadows. 'And how do you know that?'

'His name is Ernie Wright,' said the stranger, and the policeman could detect a faint Scottish burr in his voice. 'I know . . . his family.'

He looked directly at Hawkins, and in the pale moonlight the stranger's eyes glowed with a catlike intensity. 'And he's been drinking with me all night . . . '

In the crowd Mollie Wilkins looked curiously at the stranger: she'd never seen the bloke before in her life, and he'd certainly not been drinking with Ernie or Lily in the Ten Bells. But she remained silent.

'Look at him,' continued the stranger. 'He's terrified: he's scarred for life. Accuse him unjustly, send him to the hangman, and think what harm you'll do to him – to his sons that have yet to be born. Or to the granddaughter he might one day have . . . '

'That may well be so, sir,' said Hawkins, disturbed at the stranger's sudden assumption of authority. 'But if you've been with him all night then maybe you'd like to tell me all about it down at the station . . . '

'I'd be more than glad to, officer. I'm always happy to respond to the urgent calls of the London constabulary,' the stranger replied.

A little too smugly, thought Hawkins. *Like he knows more than he's letting on . . .*

'Shall we go? I believe Bishopsgate is only a few minutes' walk away . . . '

'Just what I was going to suggest,' harrumphed Hawkins, eager to reassert his authority.

'We must be getting on then,' said the stranger. 'It's late, and I've business in Soho, and then somewhere else, a long, long way from here.'

'And whom might I be addressing?' Hawkins asked.

In the darkness the stranger smiled.

'Smith,' he chuckled. 'John Smith . . . here's my card.'

A likely story, thought Hawkins, as he took the stranger's proffered business card, and slipped it into his wallet. *We'll see who he really is when we get back to the station.*

But Constable Reggie Hawkins never did arrive at Bishopsgate police station with John Smith. Somewhere along the way John Smith and Ernie Wright simply disappeared, and all Constable Hawkins remembered was that he had waved the Scotsman a cheery goodnight after directing him on to Dean Street in Soho.

And something else too. John Smith had proved conclusively to Hawkins that Ernie Wright couldn't have been responsible for the murder of Lancashire Lily. After all, all three of them – Smith, Wright and Hawkins himself – had been drinking in the same pub when the murder occurred.

Hadn't they?

Chapter 2

London, 7.15 a.m., Thursday 15 April 1909

The great bells of Big Ben tolled the quarter-hour as dawn broke over London, the imperial capital of half a planet, centre of the greatest empire the world had ever known.

Already people were hurrying off to work, streaming down the arteries of the financial, political and cultural centre of the planet; on the streets of the great city new-fangled omnibuses and motor cars rattled along, startling the horses which drew the carriages, and the unwary pedestrian. The air was full of the buzz of Englishmen and women, blissfully certain of their wellbeing and their undeniable superiority over every other race on the planet.

So intent were people on going about their business that no one stopped to look over the walls of the Victoria Embankment to notice the slim figure standing on the shores of the Thames at low tide.

Should anyone have looked, they would have wondered why such a well-to-do young woman, dressed in the latest fashions from Paris (a cream crêpe-de-Chine dress, over which was a long woollen ankle-length overcoat trimmed with chinchilla, and a dark-green velvet hat), would have been sloshing around in the mud and the rain, staring intently at a battered old blue box.

Professor Bernice Summerfield sadly reached out a hand and touched the double doors of the TARDIS. She sighed.

Nothing. No comforting response: no vibration, no hum, no warmth, no indication of what she should do next. Nothing. Just a shattered old blue box, whose paintwork was peeling, and whose woodwork was long since warped and rotten.

A few more weeks left out here in the wet and it would fall apart, destroyed by England's merciless climate when once it could have withstood even the withering energies of the Time Vortex itself.

The old girl had been through a helluva lot, thought Bernice, and now the aeons were catching up with her.

'Damn this country!' she cursed and looked up at the gathering storm clouds over the Houses of Parliament which overlooked the Thames.

She clutched at the key which hung on a chain around her neck and which the Doctor had given her two months ago.

Two months ago. Before the TARDIS had crashed and left her stranded in this Godforsaken century.

But what was the use? The lock of the police box was already rusted over and even if she could have managed to turn the key in its tarnished lock all she would have found inside would have been a small enclosed space, barely capable of holding three people, and, if she was lucky, a telephone with a direct line to the police station in the Totters Green district of Shoreditch. A police station which hadn't even been built yet.

The spacious control-room, the laboratory, the cinema, the conservatory, the Doctor's and her collection of antique bric-à-brac, the miles of corridors which went nowhere, the seemingly infinite time machine which the small box should have contained was gone, gone forever, as irretrievable as the millions upon millions of lives lost on the Seven Planets.

'Damn you, Doctor,' she cursed again. 'What in heaven's name are you playing at?'

'Benny, I want you to have this.'

'A bunch of keys? What secret doors do they unlock then?' Benny asked flippantly, as she turned away from examining the navigation panel of the TARDIS's six-sided central control console.

The Doctor frowned and he stared at Benny with that intense, knowing look that she hated, but from which she could never turn away.

'This is a key to the home of a very dear friend of mine,' he said, indicating one particularly antique key, to which had been tied a paper tag, with an address scrawled on it.

'And this –' here he pulled another more elaborate key out of the bunch – 'will open the doors to a London bank . . .'

'Somehow I can't see you saving for a rainy day, Doctor,'

she riposted.

'Indeed.' He chuckled. 'In the middle of the tornado, why bother about the odd shower?'

He looked over to Ace, who was reading the first issue of Soldier Of Fortune *magazine, instead of the nineteenth-century French novel he had recommended to her. Lying back on a Louis Quatorze* chaise-longue, *his old and trusted friend looked totally incongruous, dressed as she was in her 25th-century one-piece combat uniform. 'Isn't that right, Ace?'*

She glared back at him, and returned to her reading. The Doctor shrugged, concerned and disappointed: there was a time when he could have expected a witty and devastating reply from Ace.

These days she was more taciturn, and certainly not as blindly trusting of him as she used to be. There were times when he preferred her as an angst-ridden teenager, he thought, rather than the self-sufficient and wordly-wise young woman she had become. He turned back to Bernice.

'And this,' he said, handing the entire bunch to her, 'this is the key to the TARDIS.'

Benny drew in a sharp intake of breath. The TARDIS was sacrosanct to the Doctor, a hidden part of him to which he allowed few people free access. To offer her the key to his own private domain was an honour indeed.

'I've given this to few people, Benny,' he said sombrely. 'One of them was my granddaughter, Susan. Like the other keys I've given you it can be used only by you or another member of the TARDIS crew. Keep it well.'

He looked back at Ace. 'I've given you your freedom, Ace,' he said in answer to her unspoken but nevertheless loud complaint. 'What more do you want?'

Still the young woman from Perivale didn't speak, but looked resentfully at Benny before returning to her magazine. No matter what game the crafty old goat was up to this time, she thought bitterly, she'd never been trusted with the TARDIS key.

The Doctor sighed. The key wasn't the problem, he realized, it was Benny. He liked the archaeologist from the 25th century, and he knew that deep down so did Ace – or at the very least gave the older woman her grudging respect. But Ace had travelled with the Doctor for so long, one half of what she'd called the 'perfect team', that she'd become accustomed to being the sole focus of the Doctor's attentions.

When the Doctor had been in trouble before, there had always been Ace to help him out. Benny's intrusion on board as a crew member had been difficult for her to accept.

That's the trouble with triangles, he thought; someone always gets left out on the sharp end.

The Time Lord shrugged: he had more important things to occupy his mind than the vagaries of the female of the human species. He began to potter around the control chamber, occasionally stopping to adjust the controls on the mushroom-shaped central console. Finally satisfied that all his checks were complete he yawned theatrically.

'Tired, Doctor?' asked Benny.

'The centuries are catching up with me,' he said casually.

Behind him Ace stared at him accusingly. Oh yeah? *she thought.* When was the last time you were tired? Sleep is for tortoises, you told me once.

The Time Lord indicated the transparent central column on the console deck. Its steady rise and fall was beginning to slow down, an indication that the time machine was drawing near to its pre-set destination.

'The TARDIS will be arriving shortly,' he said.

'Where?' asked Ace.

'Blackpool? The Eye of Orion?' he suggested. 'I told you it's time to get away. I need a holiday.'

He turned to Benny, as if struck by a sudden important thought. 'Benny, you do know how to materialize the TARDIS, don't you?'

Benny was surprised. 'You never showed me,' she said.

'Well, now it's time to learn!' he announced grandly, and began to instruct Benny in the landing procedures of the time machine, flicking this lever and depressing that touch-sensitive control.

Benny watched carefully, with the intensity of a scholar eager to remember each and every one of her mentor's instructions.

On the chaise-longue, *however, Ace frowned; not because the Doctor had never instructed her in the landing procedures –*

she realized that he knew that she'd sussed that out for herself ages ago, just by watching him – but because there was something not quite right.

She looked at his back: the rhythm was all wrong, the arms were going in different directions, in different sequences; he was checking this control when he should have been checking that LED display, and adjusting controls on the navigational panel when he should have been shutting down that system on the life-support control bank.

She realized that he wasn't instructing Benny in any landing procedures that she knew.

'I'm going to bed,' she said, and threw her magazine to the ground. When no one responded she announced the fact even more loudly.

The Doctor turned around. 'It's not like you to miss a landing, Ace.' When she didn't reply he said: 'Well, good night then, Ace.'

There was a reluctant flash of understanding between the two old fellow travellers, the compliance of two unwilling conspirators. The Doctor knew that he'd been found out; but he also knew that Ace wasn't going to betray him to Benny.

After Ace had left the console room, the Doctor returned to instructing Benny in the operation of his time machine. When he had finished his instructions, he looked up at her.

'Now, you can remember all that, can't you?'

'Of course,' said Benny, and ran through the sequence with him again.

The Doctor clapped his hands triumphantly. 'Good! I knew I could rely on you, Benny!' He gestured expansively around the control room. 'Then all this is all yours,' he said, and moved to the door which led into the interior of the TARDIS, and his own quarters, the location of which had never been revealed to either Bernice or Ace.

'Doctor, are you really going to bed?'

'Of course. You can land the TARDIS while I rest . . .'

He gestured to an LED display which was flashing on one of the console's six panels. 'Twenty minutes to go,' he said. 'Guide her in safely, won't you?'

And with that the Time Lord left the console room.

Benny stared at the door for a time, wondering. There had been something odd about the Doctor's manner for a long while, she thought. He had been more stand-offish and distant than ever before, not just with her but with Ace as well.

And now this apparent volte-face, *entrusting her with the running of the TARDIS. It only served to remind her of the fact that he was an alien, from an unimaginably distant culture, who led his life according to a violently different set of moral guidelines.*

And he was getting untidy in his old age too, she tut-tutted as she noticed an old cardboard shoe box which had been dumped by the eagle-shaped lectern by the main doors, one of several antiques the Doctor had recently dusted down and returned to the console room.

She crossed over to the box and, with the innate and guilt-free curiosity of the archaeologist, bent down to rifle through its contents. They seemed to be memorabilia from one of the Time Lord's trips to Earth, and that in itself was strange because she'd never thought of the Doctor as the sentimental type.

A bag of heavy copper coins she recognized as old pennies, stamped with the unsmiling bearded face of King Edward VII, and some large old-fashioned five-pound notes; a couple of letters written on fine vellum, one bearing the address of a London bank, the other a private address; and the business card of a bookshop, also in London.

'So what do you think, eh?' she asked the carved mahogany bird.

When no reply came she stood up, and for the first time noticed the long ebony bar set into one of the roundels at eye level, above the cardboard box. She frowned: she was sure that it had never been there before.

That was one of the most worrying things about the TARDIS; able to alter infinitely its interior dimensions, it frequently did just that. Corridors which once led to its spacious and eclectic library, or the art gallery, would suddenly turn into dead ends, and rooms of fine antiques she would suddenly find jettisoned for no apparent reason.

Almost as if the TARDIS was a living, thinking being, she thought, constantly upgrading and redefining itself.

She examined the bar more closely.

Apart from two golden knobs at each end which fixed it to the wall the bar was deepest black, inlaid with gossamer threads of silver and gold which twinkled and pulsed warmly in the harsh cold light of the console chamber.

About fifteen inches long, it reminded Benny of the magic wands of the old conjurer her mother, Claire, had taken her to when she was seven years old. When she ran her hand down it, it tingled, and she pulled away, as if she had been given an electric shock.

Before she could examine the bar more closely a sharp ting! *from the control console told her that the TARDIS was coming in to land.*

She rushed over to the console, to check the instruments, and her hand flicked over the controls as she followed the Doctor's instructions for landing the time machine.

As she initiated the final sequence of commands she was dimly aware of a deep, repetitive booming sound coming from somewhere deep within the TARDIS itself; like the tolling of a heavy cathedral bell, she thought.

What was it Ace had once said about a bell in the TARDIS? A sign of impending danger . . .

She sniffed the air; normally antiseptically clean, now there was a faint acrid odour in the chamber – like mercury, she imagined.

She glanced over instinctively to the ebony bar on the opposite wall. The filigree streaks of gold and silver were dancing wildly now, almost expectantly, in its blackness.

Well, what the hell? I can worry about that later, *Benny thought, and pulled down the final lever.*

Interlude

The terrace of the House of Commons, London
7.35 a.m., Thursday 15 April 1909

'She's there again,' said Edwin Rutherford, MP for Mummerset West, who was sheltering under a large black umbrella. 'Almost every day for six weeks now. What is she about?'

He turned to his companion, a tall but corpulent man, almost completely bald, who was watching Benny on the bank of the Albert Embankment opposite with dark piercing eyes. Dressed in a long woollen coat which reached almost to the ground, he seemed oblivious to the wind and the driving April rain. A sense of power hung around him, as though he were defying the elements themselves to harm him.

'There's no need for you to know,' he replied. His voice was dark and detached, as though he regarded the grey-haired old man by his side of little importance to him.

'Damn it all, Khan,' blurted Rutherford. 'I think I should be told!'

Khan turned to Rutherford and fixed him with a dangerous look. Rutherford quaked: had he gone too far? He knew the rumours about his companion, about the ways he exacted revenge on those who thwarted him; the sexagenarian MP wasn't to know that those rumours had been spread by none other than Khan himself.

But when Khan spoke, it was with a friendly and relaxed tone, and Rutherford breathed a heavy sigh of relief. 'What we are doing, my dear friend, is all for the Higher Purposes of the New Dawn,' he said, as if that would explain everything.

'But the young lady down there?' he asked. 'The blue box? What is it?'

'Let us say the blue box is a – sacred curiosity,' smiled Khan. 'That is why I have asked you, as a Home Office minister – and, above all, as a member of our Sacred Order of the New Dawn – to arrange a discreet twenty-four-hour police guard around it, to discourage all but the young lady from interfering with it.'

'But our resources are stretched as it is,' Rutherford complained. 'If Mr Asquith, or His Majesty, heard about this waste of our resources at such a time, there would be a massive public outcry.'

Khan arched a finely plucked eyebrow in interest. 'There has been another killing?'

Rutherford showed him the front page of the *Daily Mail*, and indicated the lurid report of the slaughter of a trader's young daughter near Billingsgate fish market.

'The third such murder this month,' he said, 'and the seventh since February.'

'And all the same?'

'Their bodies cut open and eviscerated. As unthinkingly and as unfeelingly as we would dissect a mouse . . . These cases are reminding the people of Jack the Ripper and how our police failed to catch him also.'

'A few common prostitutes, low-lifes and runaways,' Khan said disinterestedly. 'Few would bother if the newspapers didn't indulge in such penny-dreadful antics to sell a few more copies.'

Rutherford stared at Khan, disconcerted by Khan's abrupt dismissal of seven young lives. 'There are some who blame the Jews, of course,' he said. 'Others attribute it to supernatural causes.'

Khan chuckled. 'Springheel Jack again, I suppose.'

'There is even a group which claims it to be the work of a secret society, such as the Templars or the Masons.'

Khan smiled. 'Or the New Dawn, Rutherford? Is that what you're trying to say?'

'Can I have your word as a gentleman that the New Dawn knows nothing whatsoever of these terrible murders?'

'You have my word, Rutherford, the New Dawn knows nothing of them,' said Khan.

Chapter 3

39 Dean Street, Soho, London,
2.30 p.m., Thursday 15 April AD 1909

Fortified by several glasses of cheap red wine she'd taken at Schmidt's Wine Lodge down the road, Benny wearily climbed the wooden steps which led up to her lodgings on the first floor of a house in Dean Street, in the heart of London's Soho.

She'd been here for two months now, ever since the TARDIS – or the police box shell which was all that was left of it – had deposited her on the muddy banks of the Thames, and she had become used to the friendly tarts who hung around the street corners, the smell of French and Italian food from the homes and restaurants belonging to foreign immigrants, and the sharp, unpolluted air, so fresh and different from that of her own dirty and grubby 25th century.

One thing she would never get used to, she decided, as she stumbled over her long mud-bespattered dress, were the damned fashions of this period. They might be OK for the ladies of leisure up in Belgravia, but for someone who tramped the streets of London each morning, trying to make sense out of the crazy mess the Doctor had dropped her into, they were as much use as a Draconian at a WI meeting.

Still, she reflected, it wasn't every day that a fashionable and expensive wardrobe and a home were provided for a girl the instant she'd arrived in a foreign time. When she had knocked on the door of the house in Dean Street her landlady had been expecting her, the kettle was already on the fire, and several dresses direct from Paris had been laid out for her on a freshly made bed.

And anyway, the wine she'd drunk, in an effort to forget her problems for a while, probably accounted for her tripping up the stairs in her long dress.

She creaked the door open. 'Margaret,' she called, 'are you in?'

Benny's landlady, a small frail old lady of seventy-eight, dressed in a long black dress, a patchwork shawl over her shoulders, came out of the parlour, and smiled at Benny. 'Come in, my dear, my guests were just leaving.'

Benny looked at Margaret's companions, grinning when she saw Matilda and Agatha, two slightly dotty old ladies, who shared Margaret's interest in spiritualism and love of more than a few nips of good malt whisky. She found them rather endearing, like minor characters from one of the Agatha Christie novels she'd read on disk in the TARDIS's eclectic library.

However, she frowned when she saw her third guest, a tall, blond, effete-looking young man, with narrow weaselish eyes and yellowed teeth. He was about twenty-six, the youngest son of a minor aristocratic family, but looked much older, the result of too much time spent in the clap- and dope-houses around Seven Dials, she guessed.

'Hello, Bellingham,' she said frostily.

Randolph Bellingham nodded a welcome, and accepted the long cloak and cane which Margaret was offering him. 'Miss Summerfield. Such a pleasure to meet you again,' he smarmed.

'I'm so glad that *you're* pleased,' she said meaningfully. The young man, who had tried to make a pass at her several weeks ago, made her shiver.

'Lord Bellingham is going to take us for a ride home in his brand-new motor car, isn't that exciting?' gushed Agatha.

'Wildly,' said Benny. 'But they'll never catch on . . .'

'Really? I would have thought that you of all people would be continually looking to the future,' the young aristocrat said.

'What do you mean?' A sense of urgency in Benny's voice.

'Why, that you always appeared to me to be an independent progressive woman,' he replied and added slyly: 'Whatever did you think I meant?'

'Agatha, Your Lordship, please hurry up!' urged Matilda who was waiting by the door. With a look of resignation at Margaret, Agatha and the young man took their leave.

Benny shuddered, and entered the darkened parlour. She could still smell the rank smell from Bellingham's cigarettes.

'Why do you mix with his type, Margaret?' she asked. 'He's about as trustworthy as a Hoothi on heat.' In response to her landlady's look of total bewilderment, she tried to find the right early 20th-century word. 'A cad? A bounder? A rotter?'

'You're too harsh, Benny. You should always look for the best in people,' Margaret chided, and opened the curtains. The early afternoon sun streamed through the window, making her fine white hair shine like a halo. *Rather appropriately,* thought Benny, *for someone who wouldn't hurt a fly and wouldn't hear a bad word said against even a slimeball like Bellingham.* Benny looked at the small card table in the centre of the room.

'Have you been playing the cards again, Margaret?' she asked. 'It's superstitious nonsense, you know that.'

Margaret smiled charitably at the younger woman, and collected up her much-used Tarot cards.

'The Doctor didn't think so,' she said. 'He said that they helped to open up the subconscious realms of the mind. That in ancient times they were a secret code known only to a chosen few. He brought me this pack when he first suggested that I move in here and look after his house.'

'And when was that?'

Margaret thought. 'It was when my poor older brother Teddy was reported missing, so it must have been 1872,' she decided. 'Such a shame that. I never did see him after that fire at his friend's house in Canterbury in '66. Affected his mind, they said. He went off to Africa, and we never heard from him again.

'I saw Victoria, his daughter, from time to time though, always with the Doctor, although there was that time when she sailed alone from Vienna where she was studying graphology.

'After her poor father's death she sold off most of the Waterfield family estate, apart from the lease on this house which went to the Doctor. She said he needed a permanent base in London, but goodness knows what for: he's hardly ever here, that's why he suggested that I look after the running of the place for him.'

'Do you see anything of your niece now?' asked Benny, even though she already knew the answer.

Margaret Waterfield sighed. 'Gone off to Argentina, she has. I get letters from time to time, but I don't suppose I'll ever see her again.'

Well, Doctor, I have to say I'm impressed, Benny thought

wryly. *Poor Margaret doesn't even know that her brother Edward Waterfield was murdered on an alien planet, and that her niece travelled with you for a while before settling down in this planet's future.*

A few trips in the TARDIS to selected points in history, a few pre-written letters posted at intervals from another country, and there might be tears, but there'll be no questions asked.

Got it all wrapped up neatly, haven't you? No sudden disappearances, no problems with the authorities, just one tidy tying-up of loose ends. Do you do that for all the people you abduct, I wonder?

'The Doctor I see from time to time, though, with news of dear Victoria,' continued Margaret. 'A strange man, but a good man, you understand. It was so kind of him to buy those dresses for you in February when he was last over, and to warn me of your arrival.'

Warned everyone apart from me, that is.

She was lucky too, that Margaret had inherited much of her brother's fortune, and didn't mind supporting her for her first few days in London. As soon as Benny had realized that she was stranded in this century she could have kicked herself for not taking the money from the cardboard box she had found in the TARDIS console room before the time machine had crashed.

She casually wondered whether the Doctor had not put it there himself for her to find. It would be just like him; she was starting to understand why Ace could often be so distrustful of her old friend. When you've been manipulated as much as Ace apparently had, you're bound to tread a little warily when the Doctor's around.

'A letter arrived for you today, dear,' Margaret said and stood up to go over to the mantelpiece. As she did so, for a half-instant she lost consciousness, and faltered. Benny was at her side instantly, but Margaret declined her support.

'Just another of my dizzy spells,' she explained. 'Nothing to trouble yourself over.'

'You've been having a few too many of those lately,' Benny said with concern, and added without any sense of irony: 'Perhaps you should see a doctor?' Margaret brushed aside the younger woman's concern, and handed Benny the envelope.

Well, at least it's not from the bank manager, Benny thought. On the fourth day after her arrival, a letter from Mr Malcolm, the Chairman of the exclusive Coutts Bank, had turned up on the doormat, welcoming her to London and reminding her that she was one of the five co-signatories to an account held since 1868 in the name of R. J. Smith Esq.

Benny had failed to make the connection until she went along to the bank's offices in the Strand out of curiosity, and discovered that her four fellow signatories were Victoria Waterfield herself, a Miss S. Foreman, a Miss S. J. Smith, and a Miss M. Bush.

The junior bank clerk had smiled knowingly at Benny, as if to suggest that he knew exactly why Mr R. J. Smith would have only young women as co-signatories to his account. But when Benny had added disarmingly, 'And no, I'm not one of his kept women,' he had blushed with embarrassment and returned hurriedly to his ledger.

So, four days into her exile on 20th-century Earth, Benny had found that not only had it been arranged that she was to be dressed in the latest Paris fashions, to be resident in one of London's more racy and cosmopolitan areas (where her odd behaviour would only be taken as typical of a certain kind of bohemian lady): but that she was also to have unlimited access to an (empty) safe deposit box, and a bank account which contained almost a quarter of a million pounds sterling.

And what blasted use is that, she asked herself, *when all the money on this backward planet couldn't buy the technology to put the TARDIS back together again?*

She looked at the letter Margaret had given her, and tried to recognize the fine cursive script on the envelope.

'From the Doctor?' asked Margaret.

Benny shrugged. 'Who else knows I'm here?' she asked. Perhaps at last the manipulating old so-and-so was getting in touch; with a bit of luck she'd now learn exactly what was going on.

She resisted the temptation to rip open the envelope, and first of all tore off the stamp and slipped it into her pocket: if she ever got back home to the future, at least she'd be able to make some sort of hefty profit at a stamp auction.

Inside the envelope she found a single sheet of note paper on which had been scrawled a map, unsigned and incomplete, as if the artist had been in a desperate hurry; and a dirty tattered playing card.

No, not a playing card, a Tarot card. She held it up to Margaret. 'You're the expert on mumbo-jumbo, Margaret. What does this mean?'

Margaret took the card from her hand and studied the colourful picture of a young man dressed in rags and carrying a bag slung over his shoulder on the end of a stick. So intent was he on following the brightly coloured butterfly in front of him that he was unaware that he was stepping over the edge of a cliff into the abyss below.

'The unnumbered card,' said Margaret. '*Le Fou* – the Fool.'

'I understand French,' Benny snapped impatiently. 'What does it mean?'

'It's both the first and the last card of the Tarot sequence,' Margaret explained. 'The card that is neither good nor evil in itself but carries within it the potential to be both. It foretells the ending of one cycle of life and the beginning of another, a time of unchecked chaos –'

'I was afraid you were going to say something like that,' Benny said gloomily. 'And this?' She handed Margaret the sketch map.

The old woman examined it for a moment. 'I'm sorry, Benny. It could be a map of the old East End – I recognize some of the street names. But I've never been there. What can it all mean?'

Benny took the map and the card from her puzzled landlady. 'Well, there's only one way to find out, isn't there?' she said determinedly. 'The TARDIS has brought me here for some purpose, and I'm tired of having my strings pulled like some damn Pinocchio –'

'Who, my dear?'

'You know, the Disney vid-disk,' she explained, blithely unaware that in 1909 the American producer of the animation classic was still only eight years old.

'Oh, I see,' said Margaret, not seeing at all. 'But what about your tea? I've some scones in the oven . . . '

Benny smiled: in the two months she'd been here Margaret had been like a kindly aunt to her, making sure she always had enough to eat, consoling her after an unsuccessful night spent in some low-life bar looking for the missing Ace; or an early morning visit to the British Museum library where, yes, the clerk assured her, Doctor Smith was a regular visitor here but no, he had not seen him for some time now.

Margaret's kindness was one of the more refreshing aspects of the twentieth century; in Benny's own century people were more inclined to shoot you first and offer you a piece of fairy-cake later.

Margaret smiled winningly at the younger woman, until Benny bowed to the irresistible pressure.

Never engage in single-handed unarmed combat with Special Weapons Daleks or little old ladies with a heart of gold, she reminded herself.

'OK, Margaret,' she said. 'You win. But after that I'm gorn down t' apple 'n' stairs, to take a butcher's at the East End manor. An' ain't that gorn be luverrly then?'

'If you say so, dear, if you say so . . . '

Interlude

Khan-balik (modern-day Beijing), Cathay, AD 1289

The young astrologer, one of the five thousand soothsayers in the employ of the great Kubilai Khan, Khan of all the Mongol people, and leader of one of the most civilized races in the planet's history, hobbled into the throne room of his master as quickly as he could.

Every day he felt a little stronger, but, even though he could now walk unaided, his legs were still weak underneath him. As he entered the magnificent chamber and kow-towed to the great prince, the Khan raised a wizened old hand in greeting.

'Welcome, my most learned of all astrologers,' Kubilai Khan said. 'Your years may be tender but of all my astrologers your predictions have proved the most truthful and the most beneficial . . . All that you have said has come to pass . . . '

The young astrologer dared to raise his head and look at his aged lord. Of course he knew that his forecasts were correct: how could it be otherwise with all the knowledge he had been given access to? But the secrets, he knew, were not in the stars; or at least not in the stars that the Khan had in mind.

The look in the astrologer's narrow eyes changed at the Mongol's words, changed from one of hope to one of victory, and then to one of desperate greed. After a decade or more of planning, his long-awaited moment of triumph had finally arrived.

'Then, may I have the guerdon which I was promised, my lord?' he asked his voice trembling in anticipation.

Kubilai Khan smiled sadly and shook his head. 'Ask one to catch the wind rather and seal it in a broken jar, my son, than to offer you the one thing that it is no longer in my power to give.'

The astrologer suddenly found it difficult to breathe: all these years of planning, of debasing himself, of insinuating himself into the Khan's confidence, to be thwarted when the prize had been so very near!

He knew better than to give voice to his real feelings but if the aged Kubilai Khan had looked closely at his servant he would have seen his eyes glow with hatred and contempt; he would have seen in that instant that his use to the young astrologer was over.

'The great Khan, however, will see that you are well provided for,' he said expansively. 'I will give you titles and lands, my son, carpets of purest silk and goblets encrusted with emerald, and jade backgammon and chess sets, fine vineyards and suppliant wives . . . '

But not that which I crave the most, and on which my existence depends!

The astrologer bowed his head. 'Then I am content, my lord,' he lied through gritted teeth, and left the presence of Kubilai Khan forever.

Chapter 4

Spitalfields, London,
10.45 p.m., Thursday 15 April AD 1909

'I may buy you another drink, miss?'

Benny scowled at the fat middle-aged man with the shock of untidy grey hair who had walked up to the bar. This was the third time it had happened in the past fifteen minutes. Couldn't a woman be left alone in a bar to have a couple of glasses of malt whisky without being pestered by overweight, middle-aged males with an abnormally high testosterone count?

Another minute and she'd forget she was a lady and give him a good unladylike kneeing right where it would do the most damage. At the very least she'd give him a thump with her handbag, which seemed to be the only sensible use this preposterous piece of 20th-century female apparel could be put to.

Behind the bar, the landlord smiled. 'Leave her alone, mate,' he said good-naturedly to the punter. 'If the "lady" wants a quiet drink, let her.'

Benny's unwelcome companion doffed his hat to her and turned a bright shade of red. '*Izvenitie*,' he said. 'Most sorry, madam.'

A Russian in the East End? Benny observed him closely as he shuffled back to his table and his glass of vodka. *Too well-dressed to be working in the sweatshops. He carries himself like someone who's used to being in charge. He's as much a stranger in this place as I am. So what's he doing here?*

The landlord regarded Benny with interest. This one was out of her element here, he realized. Them fancy clothes she wore would have cost any of the local girls a year's wages, and that phoney Cockney accent didn't fool him for a minute. She was a nob, there was no doubt about that; so what was she doing in here?

Maybe she was one of those crazy suffragettes, determined to prove her so-called independence by being the lone woman in a pub full of men. Or more likely an interfering social worker, out to save fallen women. Well, she was in the wrong place for that, he reflected; the girls on the game frequented the pubs round Commercial Street, or at least they did until the recent spate of murders.

Benny continued to sip at her drink, trying to ignore the muffled conversations all around her, every single one of which was about her. She showed the map to the landlord.

'Know this part o' the manor, mate?' she asked.

He squinted at the map, and the street marked with an 'X'. 'Wentworth Street? It's five minutes' walk from here,' he said and gave her directions. 'Let me give you a word of advice, miss – er, what did you say your name was again?'

'I didn't,' she said.

'Go back home, love, this ain't the place for the likes o' you.'

'What d'you mean?'

'Look, you're a woman. Stay at home where you belong . . . '

That did it. Benny smiled sweetly at the landlord: it was the sort of smile that in five centuries' time would give any number of interplanetary warlords cause for immediate concern. Now she just contented herself with a few reasonable words.

'And you're an interfering antediluvian chauvinist with a bad case of eczema, who waters down his gin, and runs the cheapest flea-pit of a tavern this side of the Magellanic Cluster,' she said evenly, no longer bothering to affect her grotesque Cockney accent.

The landlord frowned: he'd understood only about a quarter of what Benny had said, but he somehow realized that he'd just been insulted by an expert.

'I don't have to stay here to be insulted by someone who'd make an australopithecus feel Science Academy material,' she announced sniffily. 'I'm a lady, I am.'

And with that Bernice Summerfield, lady, stalked out of the pub, leaving the entire clientele speechless.

In the corner the Russian put on his hat and stood up from his table, following her.

* * *

This is ridiculous, thought Benny, *walking in a darkened alley-way like a bloody whore*. What do I do if someone stops me? Did they have credit cards in this century?

She had to admit that she had no idea what she was searching for. But as the Doctor had so often said, I'll know when I find it. And the map she had received this afternoon had been the first definite clue in her two-months' stay in London. The map had to have come from the Doctor, she reasoned with herself; and if that was so he must have wanted her to come here tonight. So where the hell was he?

Or maybe she was wrong and he wasn't going to put in an appearance after all. Maybe he was back in Dean Street at this very moment, sharing a fireside chat with Margaret and laughing at how she'd been sent out on a wild-goose chase. Well, whatever it was, she was going to find out what the hell he was playing at if it was the last thing she ever did.

Which it might well be, she thought. Though not as battle-wise and instinctive as Ace, Benny had been on her own since her early teens and she had developed a finely tuned sense of danger. And that sense of danger was ringing out loudly right now.

She glanced behind her nervously: the fog was coming in fast and the spluttering gas lamps in the street didn't offer her enough light to feel happy with. If only she'd had a solar-powered torch or even a pack of the Doctor's ever-lasting matches, but the only anachronism she had allowed herself in this century were her boots which were echoing loudly – much, much too loudly – in the damp and cobbled street.

She increased her pace, heading towards Commercial Street, where the porters and traders at Spitalfields market were beginning to arrive for the night's work.

A black shape leapt out of the shadows and flung itself at Benny, knocking her to the ground with a *thud!* and sending her handbag flying. For a second she was dazed, aware only of the heavy bulk of her assailant on top of her, his large hairy hands reaching for her throat. She clawed desperately at his face, but he ignored her blows as an elephant would an irritating fly.

Damn these clothes! Benny cursed as she raised her knee, ripping her dress in the process, but succeeding in giving her attacker a savage blow in the groin.

He squealed with pain, but his hands did not relent in their pressure around her neck. Benny struggled wildly beneath his weight but his strength was too great even for an expert fighter like herself. She began to feel dizzy, and the pulse in her temple pounded furiously when, from somewhere far off, she thought she could hear the sound of footsteps running down an alleyway.

'Unhand her, you villain!'

Oh great, I've died and ended up in a 20th-century melodrama! she giggled nervously to herself.

Her attacker suddenly leapt to his feet and, unwilling to fight or be recognized, ran off down the alleyway. Benny felt a pair of chubby hands helping her to her feet.

'Madam, are you quite all right?'

The voice was solicitous – and Russian. Through fogged eyes Benny looked up at the face of the fat Russian who had offered her a drink in the pub earlier.

'Thank you,' she gasped.

The Russian took a small flask of whisky from out of his overcoat pocket, and offered it to her. As she took a long grateful swig, he asked: 'You are unharmed?'

Benny nodded. 'The old windpipe's bruised: I won't be singing contralto in the choir for a while,' she said, rubbing her neck. 'But other than that I'm fine – just a bit dazed.'

'Times are becoming ever more and more violent,' the Russian tut-tutted, 'when a young lady can't even walk the streets without fear of being assaulted in the most horrific way.'

Benny shook her head. 'He wasn't interested in rape,' she said and smiled. 'And after that kick I gave him I doubt he'll ever be interested in it again.'

The Russian picked up her handbag and handed it back to her. 'Then perhaps your money?' he suggested. 'You are carrying a great deal of it around.'

'How do you know?' she asked sharply, suspiciously.

'I saw it in the tavern when you paid,' he explained. 'So did most of the other drinkers there. That is why I followed you: I feared for your safety.'

And I'd vouch that wasn't the only reason, you randy old goat!

'And it wasn't my money either; he could have easily taken

that.' Suddenly, fearing the worst, Benny shot a hand up to her neck and began unbuttoning her high-collared blouse.

'My dear young lady, I . . . ' said the Russian with embarrassment, although Benny noticed that he didn't avert his eyes from her bosom.

Benny heaved a sigh of relief. 'Thank God, it's still there.' She saw the Russian's confused expression and pulled out the chain which she'd worn around her neck since first arriving in London. 'This is what he was after.'

Attached to the golden chain were two keys: the key to a safety deposit box at Coutts Bank, and the key to the TARDIS.

'Keys?'

'Who knows what secret doors they might unlock?' she muttered to herself, and dismissed the Russian's suggestion that they contact the police.

'Then, at the very least, let me escort you home,' the Russian volunteered.

Benny studied the fat, tiny Russian. He'd obviously taken a shine to her, but he seemed harmless enough, quite endearing in a bumbling sort of way. And he might possibly have saved her life.

'My mother told me never to speak to strangers,' she pointed out.

'Then allow me to introduce myself,' he said, and bowed a courtly bow. 'Mikhail Vladimir Popov at your service!'

'In these bloody clothes I should be called Eliza Doolittle – but you can call me Benny.' Before Popov could say anything, she stopped and bent down to pick up something from the cobblestones.

'What is it, Miss Eliza – I mean, Miss Benny?'

'It's a business card. That thug must have dropped it in the fight.' She read the name on the card: '*Jared Khan, Antiquarian Books, 31½ Museum Street, Bloomsbury.*'

'Was that the villain?' asked Popov.

Benny shook her head. 'That Neanderthal couldn't read if his life depended on it. He was just a hired hand.' She slipped the card into her handbag, indicating that she would worry about it later.

'C'mon, Misha,' she said brightly, shocking – and delighting

– him by using the familiar diminutive of his name, and taking his offered arm. 'Let's go and get us a drink . . . And then you can tell me what a nice boy like you is doing in a place like this.'

'Misha, I'm sorry . . . ' Benny reached out a sympathetic hand to Popov as they sat in the dining room of the Great Eastern Hotel where the Russian was staying. The bumbling and flirtatious Russian seemed suddenly a much more tragic figure.

'*Nitchivo*, it doesn't matter,' he said to Benny, as a waiter came up to their table and brought them two more drinks. 'My little Natasha has been gone for nine months now, but she still lives on in my mind.'

'And they never caught the murderer?' Benny asked softly: she knew too well how it felt to lose someone, and the aching feeling of emptiness when you're left alone in the world.

'How could they?' asked Popov. 'No one witnessed the murder and no clues were left at the scene of the crime. For all our police could do the murderer might have vanished into thin air. Natasha had a great future – she would have studied Political Science at University – she had even met the great Lenin himself in 1907 . . .'

'But Misha,' Benny began tentatively, unwilling to remind the Russian of his grief, but still eager to hear his story, 'you said that it was because of your daughter that you came to London?'

'*Da*,' he replied, and his voice was harder now. 'Natasha was just one in a succession of young girls brutally slaughtered and thrown into the Neva River, or just left out in the streets.'

'A serial killer in St Petersburg?'

'Five murders in August alone,' he said grimly. 'And then three more in Moscow the following month.'

'But how can you tell it's the work of one man?' she asked, and recognized in Popov's eyes the glazed glint of an obsession.

'None of the girls was raped –' he pronounced the word uneasily in the presence of a 'lady' – 'and nothing of any other value was taken from their persons. But they were all cut up, and their remains examined, as precisely as we might cut up a rat for scientific purposes.'

'Hold on a minute, wasn't there something similar which happened around here a couple of days ago?' Benny asked, remembering an article she had read in one of the scandal sheets she would occasionally manage to sneak past Margaret's disapproving frown.

'Five days ago a young woman was found butchered in exactly the same way in one of the alleyways near Spitalfields market,' he said. 'It was the eighth such murder since February when a young, er . . . lady of the night –'

'The word's *whore*, Misha,' she said helpfully, and smiled, in spite of herself, at the Russian's embarrassment.

'When a young girl known around here as Lancashire Lily was attacked and slaughtered.'

'That's right: the locals are saying it's the doing of Springheel Jack,' she recalled. 'Who do you think it is, Misha?'

'One man or a thousand, I do not know,' he announced icily. 'But what I do know is that the killer of my daughter, and of scores of other people's daughters, has left the Motherland, and is come to London. And if it costs my life I intend to find him and bring him to justice.'

Benny was silent for a moment, impressed and shocked by the Russian's change of manner. There was a frightening intensity in Popov now. No longer was he a randy old goat on the make: in his search for his beloved daughter's killer he would make a formidable and tireless adversary. Benny found herself warming to him even more: not out of any sympathy, but because Popov was a fighter and Benny, like Ace, admired fighters.

Suddenly Popov grinned. 'But I bore you with my problems, *niet*?' he said, and looked down at Benny's empty glass. 'I can buy you another?'

Benny was about to say that she'd probably had enough excitement and alcohol for one night when the doors to the dining room crashed open. A wild-eyed young waiter, just arrived for work, rushed in. The maître d' rushed up to him, eager to usher him out of the room, but the young man just panted and cried out to the assembled diners:

'Springheel Jack! Springheel Jack's back!'

Chapter 5

Spitalfields, London, 00.24 a.m.,
Friday 16 April AD 1909

Benny and Popov rushed out of the hotel and followed the small cluster of people streaming into a tiny alleyway behind the hotel, just by the side of Liverpool Street railway station. With a speed and vigour totally belied by his corpulent figure, Popov raced after them, and Benny, conveniently forgetting that she was supposed to be a lady, unceremoniously hitched up her 20th-century skirts and ran after him.

'Blasted ghouls!' hissed Benny as they pushed their way through the crowd of onlookers, all hoping to see the gory and still-fresh and steaming remains of yet another victim of Springheel Jack. These were the sort of perverts who turned up in their hundreds to watch public executions, she decided, or in a later age caught the next fastline halfway across a planet to gloat over the hapless victims of the latest Spacefleet accident. Human nature doesn't change, no matter what century you find yourself stranded in.

Amazingly the woman was still alive, but thrashing about in agony on the cobblestoned floor, shuddering and clawing at her bared breasts, oblivious of the blood-curious crowd. Her fine cream-coloured coat was ripped and smeared with blood, and her face was blackened and sore. Benny darted down to her side, and examined the wound in her side.

'There's a lot of bleeding,' she said, glancing up at Popov. 'But she's hardly been touched at all. The bastard who did this must have been interrupted.'

Benny ripped off a piece of her own dress and pressed it down on the wound on the woman's side. She coughed. 'What's that bloody smell?'

Popov sniffed the air. 'Ammonia?' he suggested.

'If the bleeding doesn't get her then she'll suffocate to death on that stink.'

Benny glared up at the fascinated onlookers with unveiled disgust. Both men and women were looking down at the scene, but not one of them was considering lifting a single finger to help: young mothers had even brought their children along to catch the show.

'Damn you!' she cried. 'Someone fetch a doctor!'

Popov knelt down beside the young woman, who was tossing and turning as Benny tried to hold her calm and keep the makeshift dressing secure.

'What's wrong with her?' the Russian asked.

'Shock, more than anything else,' she replied and added sardonically, 'Hardly surprising when someone's just had a go at ripping your guts open.' She returned her attentions to the woman. 'You're going to be fine, darling, just relax, that's all. Help's coming.'

The woman grabbed Benny's arm urgently, and Benny tried to hear what the woman was saying: she had to press her ear close to the victim's mouth to make any sense of the words. When Benny raised her head she gave Popov a strange and mystified look.

'What is it, Benny?'

'It's crazy, Misha. She says she was attacked by . . . by the devil himself . . . '

She stood to her feet and addressed the crowd: 'Who is she?'

The crowd turned their faces away and muttered amongst themselves: suddenly they had no wish to get involved.

'Damn you!' Benny exploded, and grabbed the nearest man in the crowd by the collar. 'Who the hell is she?'

'It ain't none of my business,' he spluttered.

Benny increased the pressure on his neck. 'If you know who she is, tell me now, or I'll castrate you!' she growled.

'She's one of them society women,' offered a young woman in the crowd. 'Come round here to see what 'elp she can give us. Serve 'er right. We don't need no 'elp from the likes of 'er.'

Benny turned away in contempt, and looked down at Popov, who was still kneeling by the wounded woman, who was calmer now.

'She has been wounded strangely on her arms,' he said, and indicated several blue-ringed puncture marks the length of her arterial veins.

'Vampires,' said one of the crowd knowledgeably.

Cretin! thought Benny.

'She fought valiantly,' continued Popov, indicating the woman's torn dress and bloodied fingers. 'It seems to be true what we in Russia say about the English aristocracy . . .'

The familiar uniform of a British policeman pushed its way through the crowd. PC Reggie Hawkins felt the bile rise to his throat as he saw his worst nightmare take shape before his eyes: ever since he had discovered the gutted body of Lancashire Lily two months ago, he had been dreading another murder on his beat.

'It's quite all right, Constable,' said Popov. 'She will survive. And a doctor has been called for.'

'What's happened here then?' Hawkins said, asking the obvious.

'Vampires,' the cretin in the crowd repeated.

'No, it's Springheel Jack,' came another voice. 'You heard what she said: "like the devil himself".'

'Well, I reckon it's the Jews.'

Benny felt her breath stick in her throat as she heard the blatant prejudice. Even though Jews formed a considerable percentage of the workforce in the East End, anti-Semitism was still rife; in the 1880s people had been more than happy to blame the Jews for the Jack the Ripper murders, or, for that matter, anything else that was going badly at the time.

'Don't you idiots realize what your kind are going to be responsible for in thirty years' time?' she asked furiously. The faces in the crowd looked at her strangely, and Benny instantly regretted her mistake.

'Well, I reckon that them two had something to do with it,' said a voice in the crowd, and an accusing finger was pointed at Benny and Popov.

'Yeah, they're foreign. He's a Russkie, and her, well, she's a weird one, that's fer sure.'

'Look at the clothes they're wearing. Couple of nobs, that's what they is. What they doin' in our East End?'

'Wouldn't be surprised if they're in league with the murderer hisself – they might even have done it . . .'

Hawkins looked suspiciously at Benny and Popov. He tried to be a fair man but he had to admit that the crowd was right: both Benny and Popov looked distinctively out of place in the squalor of London's East End.

'And just what might you and this young lady be doing around here, sir?'

'Look, this is ridiculous,' interrupted Benny, before Popov even had the chance to explain. 'We weren't even here when she was attacked: we were drinking in the hotel . . . '

The crowd grumbled angrily; they had found a scapegoat and they weren't going to let go of it without a fight. If the police suspected these two toffs at least that meant that they'd leave the East Enders alone and wouldn't go prying into their affairs as they had at the time of the other Springheel Jack murders.

'That don't mean you couldn't have done 'er in first, though, does it?'

' "Done 'er in?" Leave off, mate! We ain't done 'er in!' Benny retorted, reverting to her fake London accent which, if she had been using it consistently, might just have gained her some credibility with the crowd. As it was, it just increased their distrust. 'Take a butcher's at her! She's breathin', ain't she?'

Popov looked curiously at Benny: there was something very odd – and indeed, in any other circumstances, rather charming – about this 'lady' who acted in the most unladylike fashion he had ever imagined, and who switched accents the way he thought only flower-sellers and professors of linguistics did. He turned to PC Hawkins.

'Your concern is admirable, sir,' he said, and reached inside his coat pocket. 'But, I assure you, totally unfounded.'

He passed an official-looking document over to the policeman who studied it and then flushed red with embarrassment.

'I do apologize, sir,' Hawkins blustered. 'Hope there was no offence taken?'

'No problem, sir,' said Popov amiably. 'You were only doing your job – and in an excellent manner, I might say! But perhaps you could dismiss these people?'

'Of course!' said Hawkins, and immediately began to disperse the crowd.

'Misha, that was wonderful,' said Benny. 'But what did you

show him?'

Popov passed the document to Benny, who frowned. 'Sorry, I can't read Cyrillic script,' she admitted. *Draconian, yes, even ancient Mondasian if I'm pushed, but not Russian!* 'What does it say?'

'Just that I am a private investigator in the service of our great Tsar, Nicholas Romanov . . . '

'Misha!' she said with admiration. 'Lawks, matey, you're the Old Bill!'

'No, my name is Mikhail Vladimir Popov, and I am only forty-nine years of age . . . '

'I mean, you're a police detective.'

'In my native Russia, yes,' he admitted. 'But here in your British Empire I am only Natasha's father.'

'Wait a minute,' Benny said, as a sudden, and eminently sensible, thought struck her. 'I know policing methods and training have changed in the past five millennia –'

'I beg your pardon?'

'Er, just a figure of speech, Misha,' she explained hurriedly. 'But I can't believe that your average twentieth-century London bobby would understand a word of Russian . . . '

'He didn't, Benny,' Popov explained. 'Attached to my identification was a translation of its revelant details. In St Petersburg I took private English lessons for five years, and my tutor there suggested that an English précis of my official papers might one day be brought to good use.'

'Ah . . . ' Benny frowned. She should have guessed. 'And your English tutor, he wouldn't be a Mister John Smith, by any chance, would he?'

'How could you know that?'

Benny shrugged. 'Oh, just a wild guess, Misha, that's all.'

After having successfully dispersed the crowd Hawkins returned to the couple, assuring them that an ambulance was on its way. Benny and Popov moved away from the woman, as Hawkins knelt down by her side to tend her wounds. Something on the ground, half-hidden in the shadows, caught Benny's attention, and she bent down to pick it up.

'What is it, Benny?'

Benny held it up to the light of a nearby gas lamp. It was

a piece of a hard greyish-brown substance, resembling a piece of bone or shell, and about as large as her fist. But even as she held it up to the light it began to crumble away in her hand.

'I'm not sure, Misha,' she replied. 'But if I didn't know any better I would swear it was chitin . . . '

'Chitin?'

'A nitrogenous derivative of glucose,' she explained, and, in response to Popov's understandable expression of total incomprehension, explained: 'The substance which forms the exo-skeleton of an insect . . . '

She rubbed away at the piece of 'bone' and it splintered and fell apart. 'But chitin is an insect's armour, it should protect it against almost anything. This stuff is as soft as soap . . . '

Suddenly a young boy, a member of the crowd which Hawkins had dismissed, ran into the alleyway, heading straight for the wounded woman on the ground beside Hawkins.

Before the policeman had time to react, the boy had dived for the woman's throat, tearing off the golden necklace which hung about her neck, and had run off back down the alleyway towards Bishopsgate.

'You little blighter!' harrumphed Hawkins and stood up to give chase.

'You look after her till the doctor comes,' ordered Benny. 'I'll catch him!' Hitching up her hated skirts once again Benny ran after the young thief.

The boy ran across Bishopsgate, and down into the alleyways of Spitalfields, where the first Springheel Jack murders had taken place two months ago. He knew the area well, and what he lacked in strength and speed, he more than made up for with his knowledge of the area. Benny would track him down to a dead-end alleyway, only to find that she had passed him by and that he was hiding in a darkened doorway, ready to run as soon as she had passed him by.

Benny, however, was stronger than him and she very soon caught up with the young thief. The young boy felt a hand on his shoulder and he looked up apprehensively.

'OK, sonny boy, you're nicked,' Benny growled.

The young boy shrugged philosophically, as though this wasn't the first time that he'd fallen foul of the law, and handed over the stolen gold necklace into Benny's outstretched hand.

'Didn't mean no harm,' he said sulkily, and his big brown eyes stared hopefully up at Benny's. Benny was only a girl, after all, he reasoned: if he played what he called his puppy-with-a-sore-paw act she'd probably let him off.

'Really?' said Benny, and her harsh tone told him that there was no way he was going to pull the wool over this woman's eyes.

'Yeah,' he said grumpily. 'She I nicked from were a toff – she ain't gonna miss one of her fancies.'

Benny looked at the golden necklace. 'It's still thieving,' she pointed out to the young boy. 'How old are you?'

'Twelve,' he said proudly, almost defiantly, as though his tender years were something to be ashamed of.

'And what's your name?'

The street urchin considered giving an alias and then looked up at Benny's face. No, there was something about this one that told him that she wasn't the law: she wasn't going to shop him.

'Charlie, Charlie Jackson, that's me name,' he said truthfully. 'Born within the sound of Bow Bells, that's me.'

'Well, Charlie Jackson, didn't your teachers tell you that stealing's a crime?'

'Never had no teachers,' he said. 'Don't want to thieve, but I ain't got no choice.'

Benny looked suspiciously down at the young black-haired street urchin, unsure whether he was giving her a line or not. 'What d'you mean?'

'You're not going to send me to prison, like?'

Benny grinned. 'No, Charlie, I'm not going to send you to prison.'

Satisfied that Benny wasn't the law, and, more to the point, that she was probably an easy touch, he suggested that he take her to his home.

Home for Charlie Jackson was a small rotten basement off Whitechapel High Street, where he lived with his mother, a woman of thirty, old before her time, and his three younger brothers and sisters. All five of them lived and slept together in one dirty and dingy room, which stank of urine and damp.

Benny found it hard to believe that human beings could live

in such squalor. Her academic studies had not prepared her for this. In the 21st century, when the results of uncontrolled industrialization became apparent on Earth, such sights were reported to have been commonplace. But in the golden age of the British Empire?

'Where's your father, Charlie?' she asked.

Charlie shoved his hands self-consciously into his pockets and stared down at the ground. 'Don't have one,' he said simply, without any trace of regret. 'He ran off to sea when I was born. Me brother and sisters don't have one either. Theirs ran off too.'

'But how do you survive?'

'Me mam works in the rag trade as a seamstress when there's work,' he said. 'And me, well, I go down to the river with the mudlarks – see what's there in the mud for me to sell . . . like that big blue box there.'

'What do you know about that?' Benny asked sharply.

'Nothing. They won't let us near it.'

'Who're "they"?'

'Coppers, like. Plain-clothes, though, wouldn't know 'em from a geezer you'd meet in the street. Mebbe they're spies!'

So there is someone else in this century who knows what the TARDIS is – or was, thought Benny. 'And you steal.'

'There ain't nothing bad about that!' he retorted and then said: 'Like I know it's wrong, but I ain't got no trade. I've got to look after me mum and the kids somehow, ain't I? I've got to provide for me own flesh and blood!'

Benny shook her head sympathetically. Charlie would probably sell his own body on the backstreets around Piccadilly if he thought it would bring in food for the family, she thought. In his circumstances survival was everything: morality was an unnecessary luxury which didn't even come into the equation.

'Charlie, if you need me, I live at 39 Dean Street in Soho,' she said. Charlie looked up glumly as if to say an address wasn't going to feed his family tonight.

Benny sighed: Charlie's puppy-dog eyes had won after all. She handed over the stolen necklace to the street urchin. Somehow she knew that Charlie would put it to much better use than the woman he had stolen it from.

* * *

It was almost three o'clock in the morning when Benny returned to her rooms in Dean Street. To her surprise the lights were still on. She opened the door to find Margaret, her eyes red-rimmed with tears. Benny rushed over to the old woman.

'Margaret? What's wrong?'

'Look around you.'

So concerned was she with Margaret that Benny had failed to notice the disarray that the flat was in. Cupboard drawers had been wrenched open and their contents flung around the room; cushions had been ripped, paintings pulled down from the wall and ripped out of their frames; even the fitted carpet had been pulled up from the floor and the floorboards underneath prised open.

'I came back from Matilda and Agatha's and I found this,' Margaret trembled. 'I feel so . . . so violated. How could anyone do this?'

'What did they take?' asked Benny urgently.

'Nothing . . . not even the money I kept in an envelope in the sideboard.'

These weren't ordinary burglars, Benny suddenly realized. *They weren't after money or antiques. They were looking for something special.*

She went into the kitchen to make Margaret a strong cup of tea. When she returned she asked Margaret if she'd contacted the police.

'The police?' Margaret shook her head. 'My dear, I've a terrible headache, and a temperature, I must have forgotten . . .'

Benny poured a tot of whisky into the cup and handed it to Margaret. She patted her sympathetically on the back.

'Don't worry, Margaret; somehow I feel the police won't be of much use in a case like this.'

'What do you mean?'

'I was attacked in the street tonight –'

'My dear!' Margaret was instantly concerned. 'Are you all right?'

'Fine. But I've now got a pretty good idea what these burglars were after.' She felt the chain around her neck. 'How did they get into the flat in the first place?'

'Who knows?'

Benny looked over at the windows, which were bolted firmly shut. 'Margaret, you did lock the door when you went out, didn't you?'

'Of course.'

Benny examined the lock of the door: there was no evidence of a break-in. 'You know, if this was anywhere else I'd say it looked like an inside job.'

'What do you mean, my dear?'

'There's no sign of forced entry,' she explained slowly. 'And who has a key to the flat?'

Margaret looked bemused, not quite willing to acknowledge what Benny was saying. 'Why, myself; and Victoria, of course; and you; and . . . and . . . '

'Exactly,' said Benny darkly. 'And the Doctor.'

Interlude

Windsor Castle, England, February, AD 1603

Elizabeth Tudor, Virgin Queen of all England, looked on fondly at her trusted counsellor and confidant. Unlike the rest of her court, who grew ever older and more preposterous, he alone seemed to retain the youth he possessed when she had first employed him in her household over twenty years before.

Some said that he had come to England from the Orient a near-cripple, but his youthful appearance and vigour now gave the lie to that assertion. With death's implacable shadow now hanging over even her, Elizabeth thought of asking him what his secret was, but the old Queen had lived too long and experienced too much to expect a truthful answer from John Dee.

'And what does your skry-stone tell you, Master Dee?' she croaked. It was an effort for her to speak now.

'Death approaches, my lady,' he admitted. 'But the throne is secure. James shall inherit the crown and the Protestant succession is assured. The glory of Her Majesty's realm shall spread throughout the known world, until another Queen, Your Majesty's descendant, shall rule over the greatest Empire this world has ever known.'

Elizabeth smiled: that was as it should be. 'Then I am content to die, Master Dee.'

She considered the youthful-looking man for a moment. 'You show much wisdom, Master Dee; never have I seen such great knowledge, never indeed since my coronation in 1559. There I met another man, a doctor of physic and other such things.'

'I have heard Your Majesty talk of him often,' admitted Dee, finding it impossible to conceal his interest. 'You have said many a time that you expected him to return.'

The Queen sighed. 'Alas, men such as he seldom keep their promises,' she said, 'even to such as I.'

Dee looked at his mistress warily. 'Then you do not expect him ever to come back to this land?' he asked, forgetting in his great anxiety to address the Queen by her proper title.

Elizabeth noticed the slight, but made no mention of it. Instead her mouth twitched into a crooked smile.

'Not to the bedside of this poor old woman, I fear,' she said. 'But I have heard that he has indeed returned to our realm.'

Dee's eyes flashed greedily as the old Queen continued: 'We have heard that Master Shakespeare has called for his advice and assistance on some new fancy of his. If anyone were to desire this doctor's acquaintance I wager that they would find him at Shakespeare's house at New Place in Stratford.' The Queen regarded Dee through saturnine, all-knowing and manipulative eyes. She affected a regal yawn. 'And now I am tired. Please leave our presence, Master Dee.' She added, almost casually: 'You have our permission to leave the court.'

'Thank you, Your Majesty,' Dee said, and left the Queen's bedchamber as quickly as respect would allow. He went to saddle a horse for the ride to Stratford.

When the door had closed behind him, Elizabeth turned towards the curtain which concealed an alcove at the far end of her chamber.

'You may come out now, Lord Doctor. I have done what you wished.'

The little man left his hiding place, but still remained in the shadows.

'Thank you, Your Majesty,' he said, in the accent of the country which would soon provide the throne of England with Elizabeth's successor.

'And why do you send Master Dee on such a fool's mission?' the Queen asked. 'He will be most displeased when he finds that you are not at Stratford.'

'The time is not yet right for him to gain what he most desires,' the man said cryptically. 'But it will come soon. And once again, Your Majesty, my thanks for giving your name to a lie.'

'It was the least I could do,' Elizabeth said. 'After all the help you gave me in 1588.'

'Just because I let Drake win that game of bowls so he could get off early?'

'And in doing so, saved our realm!' The Queen laughed and then was suddenly serious: 'What Dee said, Lord Doctor, was it true?'

The Doctor walked over and laid a bold and reassuring hand on hers. 'Everything, and more. The succession is assured for at least another four centuries, Your Majesty.'

'And after that?'

'Aha . . . '

Chapter 6

Coutts Bank, 440 Strand, London
1.30 p.m., Friday 16 April AD 1909

Benny was always impressed by the considerate and good-mannered service afforded her by the frock-coated, wing-collared clerks at Coutts Bank. This was the England she'd always heard about, before the wars and the great love plague and the CyberWars and the Daleks came, an England which up to now she had suspected had never really existed.

When she had first entered the bank she had the strongest suspicion that the staff were actually making fun of her, but in time she realized that their old-fashioned – even for 1909 – courtesy, and respect for her as a lady (albeit a lady with access to a fortune of nearly a quarter of a million), was genuine.

It was a way of life which would be mercilessly stamped out by the Great War which she alone on this planet knew would come in five years' time; but for the moment Benny was rather enjoying all the attention.

A short roundish man came out from behind the rows of banking counters and welcomed her. There was a worried look on his face as he invited her into the chairman's office.

'Miss Summerfield, you know that we at Coutts pride ourselves on the secure service we give to all our account-holders –' he began.

'Get to the point, Mr Malcolm,' she interrupted with a directness learnt in the military academies of the 25th century.

'I assure you you have nothing to worry about,' the chairman said, nonplussed by Benny's forthrightness. 'But I regret to say that there was an – incident – yesterday.'

'What sort of incident?'

'There was an attempt to gain access to your account and safety-deposit box –'

'By a man?' *The Doctor?*

'No. A woman, it seems, who was masquerading as your good

self. Fortunately my clerk saw through the deception – the woman was much older than you, Madam – but the culprit had vanished before the constabulary could arrive.'

'So nothing was taken?' When the bank chairman confirmed this she clapped her hands and stood up. 'Well, then there's nothing to worry about, is there?' she said, worried. 'Now I'd like to inspect my safety-deposit box . . . '

After Mr Malcolm had left the small private room and shut the door, Benny took the key off the chain around her neck, and inserted it into the lock of the safety-deposit box.

When she had first come to the bank one of the clerks had remarked that not only was it unusual for a client to have a strongbox which was never used, it was also odd that the client had supplied his own box, rather than one of those provided by the bank.

Not so unusual, thought Benny, *when you realize that the box is made of duronite, an alloy of machonite and duralinium which will only be invented in about four hundred years' time. If anyone wanted to break into the box before then, they'd have to discover nuclear fission first.*

She turned the key in the lock and opened the box, breathing more easily as she saw that its contents were still safe. Wrapped in a swathe of velvet was the only thing, apart from the police-box exterior, which remained of the TARDIS: a slim ebony bar, whose silver and golden filigree no longer sparkled and twinkled as it had done when Benny had first noticed it in the TARDIS console room.

On that wet and foggy February morning when the TARDIS had lurched into being on the banks of the Thames, Benny had awoken in the darkness with a debilitating headache. Though she could see nothing in the blackness, she had an overwhelming and unaccountable feeling of claustrophobia, and as the morning light poured slowly in through the TARDIS's dirty windows – *windows?* Benny thought. *What windows?* – she knew the reason why.

The TARDIS had gone, deserted her, ejected her, like a living healthy body would reject a dangerous virus. All she was left with was the cramped wooden box which the TARDIS had chosen as its exterior appearance.

As Benny staggered to her feet, she felt a gentle tingling in her hand. She looked down and found she was clutching the long ebony bar from the TARDIS, pulsing silver and gold in the shadows.

How it had got into her hand, and why it, alone of all the TARDIS, had survived the 'crash', she didn't know. All she really knew was that it was important, and when she had learnt that she had access to the Doctor's safe at Coutts, she had immediately deposited it there.

Benny ran her hand along the length of the bar. There was no tingling now: it was as cold as bone, but with a curiously clammy feel to it.

Was this what the mysterious imposter had been after yesterday? And if so, how did she – or whoever was employing her – know of its existence, and to what use was she planning to put it?

She wished the Doctor, or even Ace, were with her now: they could tell her, they would know. Benny had always left all the running of the TARDIS to the Doctor, causing him to remark once that he'd sometimes appreciate it if she'd treat him like more than just her coach driver and intergalactic tourist guide.

Ace, however, with her interest in technology, was continually poking her nose into places where it was likely to get bitten off, and Benny suspected that the girl from Perivale knew much more about the workings and secrets of the TARDIS than she cared to reveal to either Benny or the Doctor.

But now the Doctor was off somewhere pursuing his own sinister schemes, and Ace was God knew where. In the TARDIS proper, that part of the time machine which existed outside the known five dimensions? With the Doctor, laughing at her behind her back? Benny hated being out of control, hated not knowing what the hell was going on.

Too many questions, too many pieces to this bloody jigsaw puzzle!

She angrily slammed down the lid of the safety-deposit box, and called out to Mr Malcolm that she was ready to leave. On her way out she drew ten pounds from her account, and hailed a horse-drawn cab in the street, and asked to be taken to an address in Bloomsbury.

* * *

31½ Museum Street was a tiny, cluttered bookshop situated in an equally cluttered street opposite the British Museum. As Benny entered the shop another customer was just leaving.

'Well, well, well, Miss Summerfield,' oozed the familiar voice.

'Hello, Bellingham,' she replied, recognizing the young aristocrat who had been at Margaret's a few nights before. He seemed even more wasted than usual and she guessed correctly that he probably hadn't yet been home from a night out in some low-life dive.

'What are you doing here?' she asked suspiciously.

'Finest occult bookshop in the country,' he said. 'But I should be asking you what you're doing here. I thought you weren't a believer?'

'Oh, I've an open mind for most things,' she said.

'Then perhaps I might invite you to dine with me at the Café Royal tonight?'

'To *most* things, I said,' she riposted and swept past the thwarted young aristocrat and into the shop.

The walls of the bookshop were lined from floor to ceiling with hundreds of volumes, some bound in fine leather, others falling apart at the seams. Benny idly examined some of the titles: there were books on Chinese astrology, histories of witchcraft, studies of Tantric meditations, books of prophecies, biographies of famous magicians throughout the ages.

Mystical twaddle, every last one of them, she decided.

Curiously dotted around the shop were also glass tanks and bell jars containing insect specimens, some alive, some dead.

The small white-haired head of a shop assistant popped up from behind a pile of books and asked if Benny needed any help.

'Yes, I'm looking for the owner, Mister Khan.'

'I am Mister Khan,' boomed a voice behind her and Benny turned to see an impeccably dressed, fat bald-headed man come towards her. He held out his hand for her to shake. It was curiously dry to the touch, as dry as old leaves.

'Jared Khan, Madam, at your service.'

As Benny introduced herself she could feel Khan's cold, dark eyes boring deep into her. She could almost – no, not almost – she could feel his eyes as a physical sensation, violating her privacy, so powerful was his gaze.

She forced herself to stare back directly into his eyes, something which probably few people had ever had the courage to do before; Khan frowned, but he was nonetheless impressed. There was something oddly familiar about the man, Benny thought, as though she had met him fleetingly a long, long time ago.

Khan smiled, displaying a gold tooth. 'And what may I do for you, Professor Summerfield?'

'Springheel Jack.'

'Ah yes,' said Khan – *without missing a damn beat!* Benny noted. 'An interesting local legend. First recorded in the early nineteenth century, though there are some that say its genesis lies much further back in time. I have a few volumes on urban folk tales which might be of some appeal to you.' He moved over to a bookcase which was creaking under the weight of several thick volumes.

'I'm much more interested in the recent revival of the legend,' said Benny, watching Khan closely for any reaction. There was none. Even the most hardened con Benny had met would have betrayed his real emotions, by an involuntary blink of the eye, or just a slight change in the way he held himself. Either Khan was a total innocent, or he'd learnt to control his body language more than anyone else she had ever encountered. And there was one thing Benny knew instinctively: Khan was no innocent.

He took a book down from the shelf and began flicking through its pages.

'An interesting case,' he agreed. 'In times of fear simple folk often attribute supernatural causes to quite ordinary – though, of course, frightful – occurrences. But I fear that these recent reported sightings of Springheel Jack are just – "mystical twaddle", I believe your phrase was.'

Khan smiled at Benny, defying her to say that he could read her mind. But Benny was as skilled as Khan in controlling her own body language. Instead she indicated another bookshelf, and ran her fingers along some of the titles: '*The New Dawn and the Qabbalistic Path of Knowledge*; *Rites and Rhythms for a Herald to the New Dawn*; *New Dawn, Old Magic*. What is this New Dawn then?'

'A brotherhood of those interested in our planet's salvation,' he said simply.

'Only brothers and no sisters?'

'I was using the term figuratively, Miss Summerfield. Man has become decadent and evil. We of the New Dawn work to eradicate all that is useless and rotten from mankind, and help man to achieve his true destiny. We search for nothing less than the Elixir of Life.'

'Try Karn then . . . '

'I beg your pardon?'

'Oh, just a little joke,' she said. 'So how do you plan to set up this great World Order of yours?'

'We have members all over the world,' Khan said. 'Many in positions of influence. When the time is right we will take over. And then there will be an end to all wars, all starvations and all sufferings. And man's survival will be assured.'

'For a man dedicated to the survival of the human race, you certainly spend a lot of time with insects,' she remarked flippantly and indicated one of the glass tanks, where a locust was basking on a branch under a small electric light.

'Insects are the oldest and most successful species this planet has ever known, and an example to us all, Professor Summerfield,' Khan said, enthusiastically. 'Even mankind hasn't succeeded in exterminating one single insect species.'

'Now that is impressive,' agreed Benny. Cockroaches, she recalled someone once saying, were the only species guaranteed to survive a thermonuclear war: there had been a lot of cockroaches in the 25th century.

'If the human race were to die tomorrow,' continued Khan, 'insect life would carry on regardless.'

'Really?' Benny didn't quite believe that assertion.

'Well, all, that is, except for three species of human lice. Insects might even become the dominant species . . . '

When Benny had left the shop, after having failed to get any further information from the bookseller, Khan went over to the telephone and asked for a number in Piccadilly.

'Vine Street police station?' he said when the connection was made. 'Get me the Chief Inspector please.' He drummed his long, finely manicured fingers on the desk until the chief inspector came on the line.

'Good afternoon, Prior, this is Khan here. I'd like to report a murder . . . No no no, you misunderstand me. It hasn't happened yet . . . '

Khan sighed with irritation at the policeman's questions. 'But it's about to –' he looked at his pocket watch – 'in, I'd say, about two hours' time.'

Two and a half hours later, Benny arrived home at Dean Street, after once again stopping off at the local pub on the corner. She unlocked the door, and staggered into the flat, throwing her handbag, coat and preposterous hat onto a convenient chair.

'Margaret,' she called out, 'I'm back.'

There was no reply. Benny frowned. It was unlike Margaret to be out on a Friday evening: it was the one night of the week the old lady usually reserved for writing letters, or doing her knitting. On a side table there was a half-eaten biscuit and a pot of tea. Benny went over to it: it was lukewarm.

Warily, Benny entered the kitchen.

Margaret was lying on the floor in a pool of blood. She had been brutally beaten around the head with a cast-iron saucepan until her skull had been crushed. There were no signs of a struggle.

Benny rushed over to her body to check for a pulse. It was an automatic reaction – but there was no way anyone as old and frail as Margaret could have survived such a vicious attack.

Benny rarely cried – in the past five years she had, in fact, cried only twice – but now she let the tears flow freely, as every single kindness the old lady had ever shown her returned to her mind.

She was only vaguely aware of a pair of strong arms grabbing her by the shoulders and pulling her to her feet.

'You'd better come along with me, miss,' said a gruff voice behind her, and she turned to see three sombre-looking policemen.

'She's been murdered,' Benny said, rather unnecessarily.

'Well, we can discuss that at the station, miss,' said Chief Inspector Prior.

Benny looked back at Margaret's body and then at the three policemen. 'Hold on a minute, you don't think that I –'

'We'll leave that for the judge to decide,' said one of the constables, in a voice which said that that was exactly what he did think.

'But what motive would I have, you cretins?'

'Motive enough I'd say,' came a familiar voice from the doorway. 'They were arguing only last night,' said Randolph Bellingham. 'Miss Waterfield accused Miss Summerfield of embezzling her of all her money.'

'Bellingham, you effeminate paedophile, that's a lie, and you know it!'

'I'm only repeating what I heard, Inspector,' Bellingham said, all innocence.

'That's as may be, sir; and you'll certainly get the chance to repeat your accusations at the young lady's trial.'

'Trial?' asked Benny.

'That's right, miss,' said Prior. 'I'm arresting you for the murder of Miss Margaret Waterfield. Take her away, lads.'

'This is madness!' protested Benny as the two constables handcuffed her.

'Don't worry, miss, you'll receive a fair trial,' Prior assured her as his two constables led her away. 'This is England, after all.'

When Benny had left, Prior and Bellingham glanced knowingly at each other. There would be no fair trial.

As members of the New Dawn they would both see to that.

Chapter 7

Holloway Prison, London, 6.30 a.m.,
Sunday 18 April AD 1909

A series of raucous, obscene caterwaulings broke the cold morning air as Benny shuddered on her hard wooden bed and woke up to the sound of her second morning in Holloway women's prison in North London. The shrieking came from the women in the cells adjoining hers, as heavy-built, sullen-faced screws bashed on their cells doors, waking them up for the morning slop-out.

Wearily, Benny dragged herself out of her cold bed, and felt around in the dark for the foul-smelling slop-bucket which had been stinking the cell out all night. Her cell door clanked open, letting in a stream of cold, yellow light from the prison landing.

'Hurry yerself up, Summerfield,' said the warder, 'you're not in one of your fancy lah-di-da hotels on the Riviera now, y'know.'

Benny sighed, and picked up her slop-bucket, joining the other women outside who were already lining up ready to empty their own buckets. One of them, a suffragette imprisoned for interrupting an official meeting of Winston Churchill, tried to convince Benny of the validity of the suffragettes' cause; Benny responded by giving her tips on window-breaking and non-violent resistance. She then staggered on to take breakfast, which might as well have come from the slop-buckets for all the taste and nutritional value it had.

As she joined the line, a few prisoners glared evilly at her. Benny was an aristocrat, they had decided, her peculiar accent was proof of that fact, and it was pointless for Benny to try to point out that she'd picked up the accent on a planet that hadn't even been discovered yet. She was the sort of person they had nicked from when they had been on the outside, the type of woman who wouldn't even look twice at them when they were begging on the street corner.

The fact that immediately on her arrival at Holloway Benny had attempted to bribe the warders with the money she had on her (and failed – this, after all, being 20th-century England) hadn't exactly endeared her to her fellow inmates.

But the worst problem was Rosa, a prisoner Benny's own age, who occupied a cell on the same landing. Rosa, with her piercing green eyes and flame-red hair, was the Queen Bee of the inmates, Benny had decided, and for some reason she had taken an instant dislike to Benny and was already turning the other girls against her.

As Benny walked over to clear out her slop-bucket, a foot was pushed out in front of her. Benny tripped, splashing the shit all over the floor.

'Tut-tut-tut,' Rosa grinned. 'You'll have to clean that up now . . . otherwise what'll the screws say?'

'You deliberately tripped me up!' snapped Benny, instinctively raising a fist to strike Rosa.

'My, my, my what a violent girl you are,' Rosa sniggered. 'Perhaps what they say about you and that Waterfield woman are true – you did bash her head in . . . '

'How did you know?'

'Word gets around a place like this,' Rosa said. 'And one thing we don't like here is them what beats up poor defenceless old ladies. Ain't that right, girls?'

A murmur of approval came from the crowd that had gathered around the two women, sensing blood.

Well, if it's a fight you want . . . thought Benny.

'Nah, I'm not gonna let you fight,' said Rosa, as though she was reading Benny's mind. 'I'll bide me time. And then one day when you're not looking –' She drew a finger across her throat. 'Croak!'

Rosa laughed sadistically and moved away with her cronies. A young girl smiled kindly at Benny. 'She's only trying to frighten you,' she said softly.

'I've been frightened by professionals who are a lot less hairy than she is,' Benny said. 'But she meant it all right. From now on I'm going to have to watch my back all the time . . . What's she in for anyway?'

'Murdered her husband,' was the reply. 'He'd been beating

her up, like, and she snapped, couldn't take it no more. Jury asked for clemency but the judge wasn't havin' it. She's going to be hanged next week – so murdering you's not going to make any difference to her.'

'Thank you for that comforting thought. But what have I done to upset her?'

The younger girl shrugged. 'Who knows?'

Benny found out the answer later that afternoon. She was lying disconsolately on her bed after an unsuccessful interview with the acting prison governor who said that no, he didn't know why Benny's appeal was taking so long, or why no one had contacted her since she had been inside. (The fact of the matter was that the 'acting' governor had burnt Benny's papers the moment she had signed them: officially there was no record of Benny ever having entered Holloway prison.)

Suddenly the door was thrust open. One of the prison warders – a particularly butch and hard-edged piece of work named Shanklin – was standing in the doorway.

'Summerfield,' she growled. 'You've got a visitor.'

'Misha?' asked Benny and sat up on her bed. Her face fell when she saw that the visitor was Rosa who waltzed into her cell.

'Sorry, darlin', it's only me,' Rosa cooed, as the screw winked at Rosa and slammed the door on them.

Benny affected a nonchalant yawn. 'Oh, it's you,' she said, 'what do you want?'

Rosa whipped a knife out from behind her back: Benny straightened up and pressed her back to the wall.

'I want your co-operation, that's what!' hissed Rosa, and jabbed the knife towards Benny's throat. 'There's a dozen girls out there who'd like to see me carve your ladyship up!'

'There's also a prison officer out there too,' Benny pointed out calmly.

'Old Shanklin? Who do you think gave me the knife in the first place?' Rosa laughed in her face. 'Now we got to come to a deal, you and me. It's a pretty face that you got: bet you've had some boyfriends in your time. It'd be a shame to mess it up like, wouldn't it?'

'What do you want?' asked Benny, her eyes frantically flitting around her bare cell for something, anything with which to defend herself.

'A bit of information, that's all . . . '

'What good is it to you?' Benny asked. 'You'll never get to use it: you're going to be hanged next week.'

'That's where you're wrong, my beauty,' crowed Rosa. 'They've promised me out if I deliver 'em the goods.'

'Who are them – they?'

'Don't you be minding that,' she snarled. 'How do we get into it?'

'Into what?'

'Don't play all coy with me: you know what I mean! The blue box!'

The TARDIS! Rosa – no, she corrected herself, *Rosa's masters – want the TARDIS!*

Benny affected a wide-eyed, fearful expression and stared nervously down at the glinting blade of the knife. Rosa waved it menacingly in her face. 'How?'

'You use the key, of course . . . ' Benny said. She had had to sign over all her possessions – including the neckchain on which hung the keys of the TARDIS and the Coutts safety-deposit box – when she'd arrived at Holloway. Obviously the officer who had taken them from her wasn't a member of the gang who wanted entry to the TARDIS and hadn't alerted Rosa or anyone else to the fact.

'And where's the key?' demanded Rosa.

Benny refused to say, but her eyes wandered revealingly up to the tiny window ledge set about eight feet up in the wall, and which provided the cell's only source of light.

Rosa shrieked with triumph, and threw Benny roughly off the bed. She pushed the bed up against the wall and stood on it, reaching for the window ledge, her hands skimming along it for the TARDIS key.

A well-aimed foot caught her full-square in the back, winding her, and the force of it sent her slamming against the damp stone wall. In her surprise, she let go of the knife and it clattered harmless to the floor.

Rosa was winded for only a second, and she spun around to see Benny waiting for her. With a scream, Rosa leapt off the bed and knocked Benny down to the floor.

'It ain't there! You lied to me, bitch!' she screamed as she fell on top of Benny.

'You were going to kill me!' Benny cried, and her eyes watered as Rosa grabbed at her short thick hair and pulled hard. She tried to knee Rosa in the groin, but the con had her legs and one arm fastened firmly to the ground. With her free arm Benny lashed out at her opponent's eyes who jerked involuntarily back, enabling Benny to push her off.

They both saw the knife at the same instant. Rosa made a dive for it, but Benny's foot crunched down on Rosa's arm before Rosa's hand reached the knife. The murderess yelped with pain, and Benny threw herself on top of her, her hands reaching for her throat.

'Now, who are they?' she said through clenched teeth, and tightened the pressure on the woman's neck. 'Who wants the TARDIS?'

'The TARDIS?' she gasped. 'Never heard of no TARDIS!'

'The blue box, you idiot!' barked Benny. 'Tell me or I'll kill you!'

'I'll be dead next week anyway,' Rosa managed to laugh.

The door to the cell opened and Shanklin, the butch prison warder, was there standing in the doorway once more. She looked nonchalantly down on the two dishevelled women. There was no trace of surprise on her face, as though cat-fights like this were two-a-penny at Holloway.

'Get up, the pair of you,' she ordered flatly, clearly unimpressed. These new cons knew nothing: if she'd been involved in the struggle her opponent would be knocked out senseless by now. She looked at Benny.

'You've a visitor, Summerfield.'

Not another one, thought Benny, but she noticed that there was a new tone in Shanklin's voice: not quite of respect, for Shanklin never showed that to anyone, but the tone of someone who has suddenly realized that she had better tread very carefully from now on.

'He's waiting in the governor's office,' she said brusquely. 'Get along!'

When Benny had left the cell, Rosa looked warily at Shanklin.

'Well?' the warder asked gruffly.

Rosa opened her hands pleadingly. 'I tried, honest, I did,' she said. 'But she wouldn't tell me. She's as hard as old nails, that one, for all her lah-di-dah ways . . . '

'The New Dawn won't be pleased,' said Shanklin. 'You know how we treat failure . . . '

'Please . . . '

The door to the cell slammed shut, muffling Rosa's cries of agony. By the time Shanklin had finished with her she was going to be eagerly awaiting her execution.

'Misha!' cried Benny delightedly when she was ushered into the acting governor's office. Popov rushed forward to Benny, his arms outstretched.

'My dear lady!' he said with genuine concern. 'You are all right? What a sensitive reflective soul like yourself must have suffered! They have been treating you well, no?'

'Room service leaves a little to be desired,' Benny remarked. 'No fine malt whisky, no Chateaubriand steak, no cute waiters wanting to be actors . . . '

'The governor here –' Popov glanced at the acting governor who glared at Benny, revealing nothing to Popov, but everything to Benny – 'has admitted that it has all been a most terrible mistake. You are, of course, now free to go, and these absurd charges against you have been dropped.'

Benny looked at Popov with genuine fondness, and planted a sloppily wet kiss on his cheek. The little Russian blushed red with embarrassment; but also swore to himself that he'd never wash his cheek again.

'Misha, I'm really impressed with you,' Benny enthused. 'I didn't realize that you had so much influence with the bigwigs in authority.'

'No no no, dear Miss Benny,' he said self-effacingly. 'It wasn't my humble self who arranged your release. It was our good friend here.'

For the first time Benny noticed the fourth person in the room: a plumpish man with wispy white hair and dressed in a smart morning suit. He offered her his hand.

'Delighted to have been of assistance, Miss Summerfield,'

he said.

Benny looked at the stranger, whose face seemed hazily familiar, and then at Popov, and then back again at the newcomer. 'Er, I'm sorry but I don't think we've been introduced . . . '

'Asquith, Herbert Henry Asquith, at your service, ma'am.'

Benny frowned. Damn it! Twentieth-century history was supposed to be one of her specialities! Why did that name ring a bell?

'The Prime Minister has been most helpful, Benny,' explained Popov. 'The moment he heard of your plight he made sure that everything was done to ensure your release.'

Of course! Asquith, the Liberal statesman and Prime Minister of Britain from 1908 to 1916.

'Thank you, Mister Prime Minister,' she said. 'It's very good of you to look after someone who isn't going to add to your Parliamentary majority –'

'Benny!' reproved Popov, quite shocked at his friend's audacity.

Asquith smiled. 'Ah, you are a supporter of Mrs Pankhurst then . . . '

'Oh, not at all, Prime Minister,' Benny teased. 'Just my little joke . . . '

'Most amusing, Miss Summerfield.'

'But how did you know where to find me?' she asked.

Asquith's face coloured slightly. 'Why, Smith, of course . . . '

'Ah . . . '

Say no more . . .

'A member of my club,' Asquith continued. 'He left a note for me, alerting me to your plight. A chap doesn't ask too many questions, you understand, but I gather he's a doctor.'

'He also plays a particularly interesting game of chess,' Benny said. *And not just with chess pieces*, she thought.

'I'm sure you've had a worrying two nights, my dear,' Popov interrupted. He took Benny's arm, and was delighted to discover that she didn't refuse him. 'But do look on the bright side . . . '

'Oh, there's a bright side to being banged up in Holloway, is there, Misha? You tell me about it!'

'At least you weren't out in the East End last night.'

'But I was planning to be there,' said Benny. 'What happened?'

'A veritable slaughter,' he explained. 'Seven women murdered, all in the space of an hour.'

'The place stinks like a charnel pit,' offered Asquith. 'And I'm sad to say that the constabulary seem to be at their wit's end. There will, of course, have to be an official enquiry.'

'So you see, my dear Benny, if you had been there last night, one of those poor girls might very easily have been you . . . Benny, what's wrong?'

Benny found that, quite out of character, she was trembling uncontrollably; her face was ashen with suspicion and doubt.

Oh no, he wouldn't have, would he? Not even him. Not Margaret . . . But . . . but I don't know him like Ace does: he's an alien, after all . . . What would Ace believe?

Of course, he hadn't, she convinced herself; not even the Time Lord would have engineered a murder to keep Benny safely out of the East End on Saturday night (Would he?)

She knew she was getting in too deep, that was it, and it was Rosa's masters – whoever they might be – who had callously killed Margaret simply in order to send Benny to Holloway, where they hoped Rosa would get information out of her.

'Miss Summerfield, are you quite all right?' asked the Prime Minister. 'Perhaps a brandy?'

'What? Yes, Prime Minister, I'm quite well, thank you very much,' she replied in a daze. 'But a brandy would be very welcome . . . I've got a lot of things on my mind at the moment, that's all.

'And the first thing – the most important thing – I've got to do is to arrange a funeral . . . '

Chapter 8

Golders Green Crematorium, North London,
10.30 a.m., Tuesday 20 April AD 1909

'Ashes to ashes, and dust to dust,' intoned the vicar, in the meaningless words he had used so many times before, and the coffin of Margaret, the last of the Waterfields, was consigned to the flames.

The only attendants at the funeral were Benny and Popov, and Agatha and Matilda. It was a shame that no one else had turned up: Benny particularly wanted to know who had released Margaret's body for burial without the legal requirement of an autopsy.

Four mourners: it was a meagre showing for almost eighty years of service to a cause she didn't understand.

Well, there wouldn't be any others, would there? Benny thought bitterly. *Bellingham's probably stoned out of his tiny mind in some Piccadilly dive by now, with a whore of whichever sex was more obliging last night; the bones of Margaret's only brother, Edward, are rotting on a planet which will someday be known as Skaro, the Death World; and, as for Margaret's only surviving relative, Victoria – well, she wouldn't even start living in this century for another sixty years or so.*

The Russian was dressed in black as was customary, but, apart from a long dark-purple sash across her chest, Benny had insisted that she wear a long white dress and coat.

'She was – is – an innocent, Misha,' she had explained. 'She'd been used all along, when all she wanted to do was to help. And now she's free. And I won't disgrace her memory by wearing black.'

'You are distressed, Benny.'

Benny bit her lip, but there were now no tears in her eyes. 'Sad, yes, Misha,' she admitted. 'But more than that, I'm angry. Angry at the scum who did this to her . . . And at someone else . . . '

'Who might that be, my dear?'

'It's for you to ask and never to know, Misha,' she said sadly.

Popov took her hand in a spirit of genuine sympathy and they walked slowly out through the crematorium gates.

As they left, Benny allowed herself one self-indulgent look behind her: not at the place where Margaret's coffin had been laid, but at the wreath of white lilies which had been sent by an absent mourner, a mourner whose identity was unknown to everyone but she.

And how far in advance did you order those flowers, Doctor? Benny thought bitterly. *So many deaths, so many people who made the mistake of crossing your path, and trusting you.*

So many people who will never return home any more. Those names I hear you mutter sometimes when you think I'm not listening: Adric, Sara, Katarina. The ones Ace has told me about: Sorin, Julian and Raphael. And the others: all those inhabitants of the Seven Planets.

So many deaths, Doctor; but tell me, just how many funerals have you actually bothered to turn up to?

She looked grimly at Popov. 'C'mon, Misha,' she said. 'Let's find a pub. I need to get very, very drunk . . .'

Chapter 9

The Ten Bells Pub, Spitalfields,
10.45 p.m., Wednesday 21 April AD 1909

'Oooo-errr, luvvy! You are a one!' screeched Benny in her best Cockney drawl as yet another man propositioned her. 'Mebbe later, eh? Let me talk with me mate first, like?'

Her accent was about as convincing as it had been the other night; but as most of the men in the pub were so drunk that they couldn't notice, its authenticity didn't seem to be important.

Through the smoke Benny could see Popov sitting in a corner, nursing a glass of vodka and trying to avoid the advances of the young girl who had invited herself to his table. Benny blew him a kiss through gaudily painted lips; Popov glared evilly back at her.

Benny resumed her conversation with Mollie, one of the whores who frequented the place. All the working girls of the neighbourhood were living in fear of the mysterious Springheel Jack; it was only lack of money for food that kept them out on the street, in spite of the warnings posted by the police on every street corner from Bishopsgate to Whitechapel.

'It happened to me best friend, Lily,' said Mollie. 'She were the first. Carved up like a piece of meat on a slaughter table, she was.'

'And you say she wasn't robbed,' Benny began, and then corrected herself: 'You mean nowt were nicked from her then?'

'Not a brass farthing, and I knows that Lil had a lot on her that night,' said Mollie. 'On accounts of a gentleman, like . . . '

'And what about them who says it's the Ripper returned?'

'Nah. Me old mam worked round here when Jack was about,' said Mollie. 'That were the work of a madman, someone who had a grudge against women. This one's different.'

'How different?'

'Like whoever's done it is all calm, like. As if he's not doing it for the thrill of it but because he has to. If you ask me it's the work of a gang. The Tongs, mebbe, or the Jews.'

'More than one murderer?' asked Benny. 'Like a secret society? Why?'

'Last Saturday. How could one geezer do in seven girls in an hour? And how come the coppers never catch up with them? He's got to have lookouts watching out for them. Either that or it really is Springheel Jack come back from hell to haunt us, and then we're all done for anyway.'

'You don't believe that, do you?'

'Mebbe not. But there's a lot of girls round here as do . . . ' She stopped and eyed Benny suspiciously. 'Look, you're the police, ain't you?'

'No.'

'You're not one of us though,' said Mollie. 'You might think that your tarty make-up and your street clothes can fool the rest but not me: I'm never taken in by appearances – that's why I've stayed out of trouble. Even when that rich toff came in t'other night, throwing his cash around like there was no tomorrow, I knew to stay well clear of him.'

'Toff?'

'A right gentleman he were too,' Mollie said. 'Belli – Belli something or other.'

'Bellingham,' said Benny grimly.

'Yeah, that's him all right. Quite a tasty-looking piece –'

If you want to catch something particularly nasty, thought Benny.

'Didn't care much for his mate though. Short, toady sort of bloke . . . '

Khan.

'What did they want?'

'What do you think?' laughed Mollie.

Benny arched a disbelieving eyebrow: Bellingham might like slumming it in the East End, but Khan? She doubted he'd ever been further east than Blackfriars Bridge in his life.

'They were asking questions, same as you . . . ' said Mollie. 'Did we believe in Springheel Jack? Couldn't it be Jack the Ripper come back?'

Benny stood up to go, and signalled over to Popov, who

hastily left his young companion and pushed his way through the smoke-filled bar to her side.

'Thanks, Mollie, you've been a great help,' said Benny.

'What about our deal?' Mollie reminded her. 'I've given valuable time talking to you. Could have been out making money.'

Benny smiled, and reached into her coat pocket. Mollie's eyes shone when Benny presented her with a five-pound note: it was more than she could hope to earn all week.

'Look after yourself, Mollie,' Benny told her. 'And spend this on something useful.'

'You be sure I will, miss!' breathed Mollie, and turned to the barman and ordered a large pitcher of gin.

Benny shrugged helplessly, and gave Popov her arm, who led her out of the pub, and into the foggy street. They began walking down the road towards Spitalfields market, where Benny promised she'd treat the Russian to a hot buttered muffin.

'It's the least you could do for me, Miss Benny,' he complained. 'It was most uncomfortable in that place. Why did I have to accompany you?'

'A girl can't go into a place like that by herself, Misha,' she said brightly. 'They might think I was on the game!'

'And what did they think when you went to the bar and left me for half an hour?'

'Oh, no problem at all. I just told them that you were my pimp!'

Popov began to protest when Benny suddenly grabbed his arm.

'Benny?'

'What's that smell?'

When Popov gave her a look of surprise, she continued: 'Like ammonia . . . ' She sniffed the air, and then dragged Popov down a darkened alleyway.

'Benny, really this is –' Popov began and then stopped. Benny urged him to stay in the shadows and remain silent.

At the far end of the alleyway, there came a curiously familiar wheezing sound. In a blur of silver and gold, something was shimmering into existence.

Benny held the trembling Russian even tighter as the figure

of the creature slowly took form, defining itself with colour and muscle. Within seconds it had fully materialized. It crouched on its haunches and looked around with multifaceted eyes; its antennae twitched in response to the clean fresh air of a new planet.

'What is it?' breathed Popov.

'An insect?' Benny guessed.

'It's Springheel Jack . . . '

'Don't be stupid! Now keep quiet . . . '

The creature made a few faltering steps forward, and Benny frowned: the creature was so weak that it even found walking a difficulty. Transporting itself into this alley from wherever it came from must have sapped it of most of its strength.

Still unaware of Benny and Popov's presence, the insect-like creature staggered closer to them. Huge gobs of saliva dribbled from its open mouth, and the stench of ammonia about it made Popov gag.

The creature tensed, and searched around for the source of the noise. The myriad pupils in its eyes dilated as it accustomed itself to the lack of light, until it finally spotted the two humans. It snarled, and crouched, ready to spring.

The sight was too much for Popov. With a wail he turned and ran back down the alleyway.

'Misha!' cried Benny and turned to see the creature advancing towards her. 'Oh, shit . . . '

Summoning up every last reserve of its strength the creature leaped onto Benny, knocking her to the cobblestoned ground. Razor-sharp claws ripped her dress and globs of acidic saliva stung Benny's cheeks. Even in its weakened state the creature was more than a match for Benny and she yelped in pain as she felt something puncture her left side.

Suddenly a burly arm wrapped itself around the attacker's neck and tried to pull it off Benny. As Popov struggled with the creature, Benny took advantage of the diversion to kick the creature full square in its thorax with both her feet. The creature gasped with pain, and fell back onto the ground, where Popov leapt on it.

They rolled about on the ground for a few seconds until Popov suddenly discovered that he was wrestling with thin air. The creature had vanished as swiftly as it had appeared. He stood up and helped Benny to her feet.

'Thank you, Misha,' Benny gasped, and rubbed her neck: she was going to be badly bruised there the following morning. 'You ran away, you bastard!'

'I–I apologize,' he spluttered. 'The sight of that thing must have made me lose my senses momentarily . . . '

'Forget it,' Benny said curtly.

'What was it?'

'Some sort of insect life, I suppose . . . But whatever it was it doesn't come from Earth.'

Noticing Popov's look of disbelief she continued: 'And wherever it comes from I'll wager that it – or another of its kind – is responsible for all the murders – both here and in Russia.'

She attempted to stand up and yelped in pain; the creature had injured her in the side. Ignoring Popov's protestations she undid the front of her dress to examine the wound: there was little blood, but two tiny blue-ringed puncture marks in her side.

'You are unharmed?'

'Nothing some iodine won't see to,' Benny said. 'Now let's get home!'

Interlude

Culloden, AD 1746

It was good to be back in his native land, the traveller thought, as he rode his horse across the moors and breathed in deep of the fresh Highland air. His quest had taken him halfway across the world, to many countries and different cultures, but the rolling hills, the marble-grey skies and the smell of the heather on the breeze were the only things that really mattered to him.

Thomas pulled on the reins to stop his horse, and looked about. An early-morning mist still hung over the moor, and he smiled as from somewhere far off in the distance came the mournful wail of the bagpipes. Then that sound was joined by another one, a harsher, wheezing groan, which thundered through the glen like the bellowing of a dying bull-elephant.

Cursing, Thomas kicked at his horse and galloped off down the glen. He couldn't fail now, not now when he was so close!

When he reached the site from which the noise had come he cursed. The glen was empty. He dismounted and went over to a spot where the grass had been trampled down, and still bore the traces of the object which had been there until only a few short seconds ago.

It was the shape of a tall blue box.

The traveller looked up into the stormy sky and wailed. 'How much longer will I have to wait? How much longer?'

Chapter 10

Bloomsbury, London,
10.55 p.m., Thursday 22 April AD 1909

'I must be mad to let you talk me into this, lady,' growled young Charlie Jackson as he climbed over the small stone wall and into the back yard of Khan's bookshop. 'Like it ain't legal!'

'I didn't talk you into it, Charlie,' Benny reminded the street urchin, as she swung her legs over the wall, cursing her long dress. 'I paid you fifty pounds – enough to help your mother set herself up as a proper dressmaker. And you're not going to tell me this is the first shop you've broken into . . . '

'Honest, miss,' said Charlie, with a note of panic in his voice. 'I've never done no thieving before!'

Benny smiled and ruffled the young lad's mop of untidy black hair. 'Don't worry, Charlie, I'm not the police.'

She knelt down to the boy's level, and watched as he produced a small wire instrument from his pocket and began expertly working on the lock of the back door. A few seconds' twisting and the door sprang open.

Benny stood up and patted Charlie on the back.

'Not bad,' she approved and added mischievously, 'for a first-timer! Come on, let's see what's inside.'

Silently they slipped into the shop, closing the door behind them. Benny went to the front of the shop to make sure that the blinds were drawn and then went over to Khan's desk to light an oil lamp. She began rifling through the drawers of Khan's desk.

'What are you looking for, Benny?' Charlie asked curiously.

Benny shrugged. 'I'll know when I've found it,' she admitted. 'Why don't you start looking for it over there?'

There seemed to be few items of interest in Khan's desk drawers, just records of accounts, and customers' orders for books. Nothing which would mark the man out as responsible in some way for the Springheel Jack murders, or the killing of Margaret.

In the bottom drawer Benny pulled out a dog-eared file containing newspaper clippings from around the world; they were all dated from the previous year, and mentioned the strange climatic changes which had been recorded around the globe. Benny mentioned this to Charlie, who grinned as he recalled the events of last June with relish.

'The sky was bright red, see, in the middle of the night, like a thousand fireworks had been let off at the same time,' he said. 'Me mam could even do her sewing by its light. People said it were the Second Coming, or the end of the world. No one knew what it was . . . '

Benny grinned. 'It was a meteorite, actually,' she said, remembering an article she had once found the Doctor studying in the TARDIS's data files.

'A what?'

'A big rock, thrown out of the sky,' she explained. 'It devastated a large area of Siberia.'

'Where?'

'Siberia! Don't they teach you geography at school, Charlie?'

'Don't go to no school.'

'Oh. Well, Siberia's part of Russia . . . ' she said, and then stopped.

Russia. Where Misha comes from. And where his daughter was killed.

Obviously uninterested, Charlie wandered over to a large table, creaking under the combined weight of several heavy books. 'These look important,' he said.

'What are they about?'

Charlie shrugged. 'Dunno. Can't read, you see . . . '

Benny came over and sat down by the table to read the titles.

'Magic?' Charlie gasped.

'Mystical twaddle,' Benny sneered, and then frowned and examined one of the volumes more closely. It was a book purporting to have been written by one Count Cagliostro and concerned the quest for eternal life. Charlie peered over her shoulder.

Benny showed the title page to Charlie, and pointed to the date, carefully spelling out the letters for him.

'MDCCLXXXIII? What's that mean then?'

'Roman numerals, Charlie,' she explained. 'This was published in 1783.'

'You know that just from reading them letters?' said Charlie, amazed. 'You ain't half clever, Benny . . . '

'No. I'm an archaeologist,' she said and slammed the book shut. 'Look at it, Charlie. For a book published over a hundred years ago, it's in perfect condition. Its pages should at least be yellowing, and its binding beginning to crack – but it's as good as brand new! Even a data disk would have started to deteriorate in that time.'

'So this Khan geezer looks after his books,' shrugged Charlie: he wished Benny wouldn't keep reminding him that he couldn't read. He wandered off and opened a door at the back of the shop, which led down a flight of stairs to the cellar below. 'Cor, what's that pong?'

'Pong?' Benny sniffed at the air, and leapt to her feet, knocking the book to the ground, as she recognized the familiar smell of ammonia. 'Charlie, come here!'

Materializing in front of them was the same kind of creature that had attacked Benny the night before. It had its back turned towards them and Benny could see the creature's third set of legs which it presumably used to leap great distances.

As soon as it was fully formed the creature began to examine its surroundings. Slowly it chittered across the room, running its claws along the rows and rows of books and papers. It stopped at the displays of mounted butterflies, examined them curiously for a moment, and then continued its inspection.

It looks confused, disorientated, thought Benny. *Like a drunk or a very old man . . .*

'It's Springheel Jack!' cried the terrified Charlie.

Alerted by the sound the creature spun around to face Benny and Charlie. Benny took a step towards it, and it snarled angrily and lashed out at her with a razor-sharp claw. It moved slowly towards her.

Charlie ran over to Khan's desk and grabbed a heavy book which he used to batter at the creature.

'Charlie, don't!' cried Benny, but still Charlie pounded away at the creature. The creature tried to protect itself but it was too weak, and as Charlie continued to hit it bits of the creature's exoskeleton began to fall off. Finally, with a groan, it fell to the floor, shattered and dead.

Benny bent down to examine the creature's remains, which were quickly turning to dust. She looked up angrily at Charlie.

'What the hell did you do that for?' she demanded.

Charlie looked bemused. 'I was saving your life, weren't I?'

Benny shook her head, uncertain what to think. She let the dust run through her fingers. 'You know something?' she said, more gently. 'I don't think it was attacking me at all.'

'Oh no?' Charlie wasn't convinced.

'It looked confused, like a scared rabbit. If anything it was more frightened of you than you were of it.'

'I weren't frightened,' claimed Charlie sulkily.

'Of course not.' Benny smiled indulgently, and examined the dry dust. She was reminded of a movie Ace had once made her sit though in the TARDIS's cinema. The one where the vampire is finally trapped in the light of the sun, and changes to dust in a matter of seconds. Time had finally caught up with him, Ace had told her.

And you can't escape time, the Doctor had explained to Benny once. It's the most powerful force in the Universe – all-pervasive, unfathomable, and highly unstable. Even with the protection of a TARDIS, travel through the Time Vortex is like trying to ride the Niagara Falls in a barrel. Rassilon knows what I'd do without the old girl to look after me . . .

She turned to Charlie who was still sulking. 'Look, I'm sorry. You thought you were doing the right thing,' she said. 'But the thing was intelligent. We could have talked to it.'

'Talk to a bloomin' overgrown grasshopper?' he jeered. 'Go on!'

Benny laughed: she supposed the idea did seem a little ridiculous. 'Come on, Charlie, we're going to find nothing here tonight. Let's go home.'

'I'm afraid that you won't be going anywhere, Professor Summerfield,' announced a menacing voice from the shadows. 'You've got yourself a little too involved . . . '

Jared Khan stepped out from behind one of the bookshelves. From the open door leading to the cellar two thugs emerged, and grabbed hold of Benny and Charlie.

'Myself and a few friends are holding a little meeting later tonight,' Khan said. 'You are most welcome to attend.'

'Do I have any choice?'

'Of course not.'

Khan smiled, and indicated that the two thugs should take Benny and Charlie down to the cellar. As they did so, Charlie kicked his captor hard in the shins, and made use of the diversion to run out through the front door of the shop. The thug made to give chase but Khan stopped him.

'Let him go,' he said calmly. 'He's only a child. Professor Summerfield has what we want . . . '

'You murdered Margaret Waterfield,' Benny said coldly. Khan seemed mildly amused by the accusation, which infuriated Benny even more. 'You murdered Natasha Popova in Saint Petersburg,' she continued.

'Who?' The name of Popov's murdered daughter meant nothing to him.

'And all those other girls,' Benny continued. 'Why are you doing it? Some sort of hang-up about women? Can't get it together so you take it out on those who reject you? You're a classic case!'

'Have you quite finished, Professor Summerfield?'

Damn it! Will nothing shatter that blasted complacency of his? He's in control here, but does he have to make it so bloody obvious?

'Professor Summerfield, I grieve for those murdered women as much as you do,' Khan said. 'If I could I would have done anything to spare them the terrible traumas they were put through.'

Terrible traumas? thought Benny. *Well, yes, I suppose you could call being carved up alive and your guts strewn all over London a 'terrible trauma'.*

She was about to respond to Khan's avowal of regret, when a sudden terrible thought struck her.

My God, he's telling the truth!

'Take her down to the cellar,' Khan instructed his two henchmen. 'We have a lot to talk about, Professor Summerfield.'

Chapter 11

Bloomsbury, London
11.40 p.m., Thursday 22 April AD 1909

'Insects, Professor Summerfield,' Jared Khan announced grandly.

'I've met quite a few in my time,' Benny admitted, trying to be flippant despite the fact that she had been tied to a chair down in the cellar of Khan's bookshop. 'Usually in bars at closing time when they've had too much whisky and think that they're God's gift to womankind.'

Khan smiled indulgently. 'They are the most successful species ever to walk this planet.'

'So you said. Drop a few neutron bombs and the cockroaches will still have a great party.'

Khan frowned. *Well, at least he doesn't know what a neutron bomb is,* thought Benny. *Which means he isn't an alien, or a renegade from the future . . .*

'For each human being alive today there are approximately one million insects,' continued Khan. 'They live and thrive everywhere – from the polar icecaps to the burning deserts, from the highest mountains to the deepest oceans. They are supremely adaptable; along with mankind they are the highest form of evolution.'

Tell that to the dolphins, she thought, but couldn't help being interested.

'But what has this got to do with the Springheel Jack murders?' she asked

'I'm not concerned with death, Professor,' claimed Khan, neatly sidestepping the question. 'I am concerned with life.'

Benny fixed Khan with a look which said: *prove it – if you can.*

'What would you do, Professor Summerfield, if you were given the chance to save an entire species?'

Benny didn't reply, but silently challenged Khan to continue.

'There is a place called Antýkhon,' said Khan. 'A place far from here where the soil is dead, and the sun's rays kill.'

Too many oil slicks, and an inordinate use of hairspray, thought Benny. *You might as well be talking about the 21st century.*

'The creatures who rule that planet are dying,' said Khan. 'They need a new home.'

'And these creatures are the ones who keep appearing in the East End? They want to colonize the Earth?'

'The Charrl need to survive, Professor. Our planet would make an ideal Hive World.'

'They're not being very successful so far,' Benny pointed out. 'Their teleportation equipment must be faulty. No sooner do they materialize than they disappear into thin air. It's worse than trying to catch a bandersnatch with a butterfly net.'

'The Great Divide is unstable,' admitted Khan. 'It shifts and changes constantly. To pass through it the Charrl must undergo terrible stresses, and their safe passage is never guaranteed.'

'Great Divide?'

'The gap between our world and Antýkhon,' explained Khan. 'It first opened last year, in Russia, enabling the Charrl to come to Earth –'

'The Siberian meteorite,' Benny guessed, remembering the newspaper clippings she'd seen in Khan's drawers. Khan's unknowing expression puzzled her until she remembered that the site of the explosion hadn't been investigated until some years after the blast.

'The energy must have been so great that it opened a rift in the space–time continuum,' she said, and was secretly pleased to see that Khan didn't understand what she was talking about. 'And now it's shifted to London?'

'The Charrl must be allowed to cross the Great Divide,' he said.

'A race of overgrown insects? Come on!'

'The Charrl are the greatest noblest race the Universe has ever known,' claimed Khan. 'Creators of beauty, respecters of creation, the race of the faithfulest friends. They have flourished for eleven thousand years, and have established the noblest society. Such perfection should not be allowed to die. To live, to survive and to prosper, that is their birthright!'

'And what about the women who've been killed?' asked Benny. 'What about their birthright?'

'Low lifes and whores,' Khan said dismissively, but Benny noticed the uncertain look in his eyes.

Khan genuinely couldn't care less about the murdered women, she realized, which said a great deal about his own respect for life; but he also had not the slightest clue as to why they were being murdered.

'What's in it for you, Jared?' she demanded. 'I may call you Jared, mayn't I? I can't believe that you're doing all of this just for the sake of a bunch of overgrown insects with delusions of grandeur.'

'Insects are the most successful –'

' "Race of creatures ever to walk this planet", I remember,' she said and eyed the man suspiciously. 'But what's in it for you?'

Khan paused a second before answering, and Benny recognized that she'd struck a nerve. There was something that Khan was hiding from her.

'Power, of course, Professor Summerfield,' he said finally. 'Power for the New Dawn to reorder the world the way it was intended to be –'

Benny cut him short. 'With you as second-in-command to the Chief Grasshopper, I suppose? You know, Jared, that somehow doesn't quite ring true. Admit it, your ambitions are a hell of a lot more basic than that.'

Khan glared at Benny. 'I do all I can to guarantee the birthright of the Charrl,' he claimed, rather unconvincingly, she thought.

'Well, you're not succeeding, are you?' Benny pointed out. 'The Great Divide is unstable. The after-shock of energy released from the Siberian meteorite must be fading. The two Charrl I've seen barely survived the trip from their home planet.'

'The Great Divide is closing,' admitted Khan. 'Within days it will have shut for good, and the Charrl's entry to our world will be forever denied. Unless, of course, it is stabilized.'

Benny flinched under Khan's gaze: the expression on his face was greedy, almost lustful. And desperate, she suddenly realized.

'For many long years now I have been in contact with the Great Queen Ch'tizz,' he said. 'Her counsellors have told her that there is only one thing which can stabilize the Great Divide. Only one thing which is capable of opening forever the gateway to our world for the Charrl. Only one thing which can guarantee the survival of their entire species.'

'And that's what?' asked Benny, although in her heart of hearts she already knew the answer.

'A simple blue box, Professor Summerfield,' Khan said. 'A blue box that, even as we speak, is rotting on the banks of the River Thames.'

Benny laughed as suddenly all the pieces in the jigsaw began to fit together – or so she thought.

The TARDIS must have known all along about the role it would be forced to play in the Charrl's invasion of Earth. If they succeeded now, in 1909, thousands of years of future history would be wiped out. There would be no Hitler; no Bob Marley; no Ace, no nitro-nine; no organized opposition in the Dalek Wars; no Benny. And that was impossible. Those things had happened. Benny herself was living proof.

'The TARDIS?' she jeered. 'The TARDIS is dead, Jared, whatever power it once had has vanished!'

'Dead?'

'She's committed suicide! She was one step ahead of you all the time! She destroyed herself so that you couldn't get your grubby little hands on her!'

Khan frowned and Benny could swear that his jaundiced face had turned white. 'No, not after all these years of planning,' Khan said, and Benny was shocked to see that, for one normally so composed, Khan's body actually began to shake. 'The Great Divide mustn't be allowed to close.'

An oily voice spoke up from the shadows at the far end of the room. 'Somehow I don't think Miss Summerfield here is quite telling the full truth.'

Benny turned. 'Bellingham, I might have known that you'd turn up eventually.'

Bellingham smiled and walked up to the bound woman, and touched her lightly on her breasts. Benny growled.

'You're a very rich lady, my dear,' he said, and in reply to

Benny's puzzled expression, added: 'The New Dawn have members in every major institution in the world, including the financial world. And you have a safety-deposit box.'

'So?'

'What's in it?'

'You mean you haven't found out yet?' she taunted. 'After having one of your minions impersonate me and try to get into it?'

'The New Dawn does not have minions, Professor Summerfield. In the world order we shall all be equal,' said Khan. 'But the person who tried to gain access to your safe was well known to you, indeed the only person you came to trust.'

'Margaret?' Benny gasped in disbelief. 'No, she wouldn't,' she whispered, but Khan's revelation of Margaret's apparent treachery had the desired effect, totally unsettling her.

'What is in the box?' hissed Bellingham, and Benny turned her face away from his breath which reeked of sour wine and tobacco.

Benny considered the young aristocrat with disgust. 'You'd never believe me if I told you.'

'What is in it!'

'A magic wand!'

Bellingham exploded and slapped her viciously. *God, he enjoyed that,* thought Benny. *He must really hold a grudge against me for constantly reminding him what an ineffectual little weasel he is.*

'I told you you wouldn't believe me,' she said through gritted teeth, determined not to let Bellingham see how much he had hurt her.

'And even if you could gain access to the box, you'd never be able to break into it. The technology you'd need won't be developed for several centuries yet.'

'She's babbling,' Bellingham said.

By his side Khan didn't say a word. Her *faux pas* about the future should have at least elicited some reaction of surprise from him; instead he continued to look at her through steely unblinking eyes. Benny instinctively distrusted people who remained silent, not revealing their thoughts.

'Then we'll just take the keys,' Bellingham said and reached for the chain around her neck.

'That won't help you either, lover boy,' she said smugly. 'Genetically coded, you see. The key will only work if I'm using it. The Doctor thinks of everything . . . '

'Khan? Is this true?' asked Bellingham.

Khan moved forward and gazed into Benny's eyes. She could feel the force of Khan's will battling her own, feel his being filter into her mind, probing around amongst the synapses and the neurons, the axons and dendrites, and sifting through her thoughts as though they were old dead leaves.

Khan moved through her memories, memories she had forgotten, and memories she never wished to be reminded of again, sorting out the clutter of over thirty years of active life.

For a single half-instant their spirits somehow interconnected, and Benny crossed through the barrier that Khan had erected around his own memories. A strange despairing sense of loss and pain washed over her like a fever, and then it was gone; and she shook herself out of the trance into which Khan had put her.

She suddenly felt very cold and shuddered: never before had she experienced such sheer psychic energy. Khan's mental powers were enormous, so powerful that it would have been child's play for him to use his powers to influence Margaret's mind and betray her. Indeed, she realized now that it was Margaret herself, and not so-called burglars, who had ransacked her lodgings in Dean Street.

Khan turned to his companion. 'She is telling the truth, Bellingham,' he said. 'The box will open to no one but her.'

'Then we must force her to open it!'

Khan smiled and looked at Benny knowingly. 'I rather suspect that it will be very hard to force Professor Summerfield to do anything.'

'We must have the contents of the box!' insisted Bellingham. 'The Charrl must be allowed to come to Earth!'

Benny watched with interest as Khan regarded his accomplice with barely disguised contempt. 'You don't really care about the Charrl's survival, do you? All you're interested in is the power they can give you, so you can indulge your foul perversions . . . '

'It's I who help finance the New Dawn,' insisted Bellingham.

'With money you squander from your father's estates, yes,' agreed Khan.

'I sometimes wonder how committed you are to the Charrl,' Bellingham said.

Khan glared at the younger man, who instantly realized he had gone too far. 'That is a dangerous thing to say,' he said coldly, and before he led the way upstairs turned to Benny.

'You will change your mind in due course, Miss Summerfield,' he said with certainty.

'You want to bet on it?'

'If I was a gambling man, yes. But before long you too will become convinced of the Charrl's birthright as I have become. I – we have waited too long to be thwarted at the final step.'

And with that Jared Khan gagged the bound Benny and led Bellingham upstairs to the bookshop, leaving the cellar in darkness.

Benny struggled in her bonds, trying in vain to loosen the knots of the rope which bound her to the chair. But Bellingham had taken great pleasure in tying the knots extra tightly and even if she wasn't in her present feverish state she knew that freeing herself would have been an impossible task.

She cursed herself. *Ace wouldn't have gotten herself into this mess,* she thought, *pussy-footing around and trying to get discreet answers to questions. No, she would have nitro-nined some answers out of Khan, and if she had found herself tied up would have freed herself in seconds with a Space Security-issued knife.* Sometimes, Benny thought, she was a little too ladylike for her own good.

She looked up through the iron grating at the friendly winking stars in the sky above. She wondered if she'd ever travel amongst them again. Khan had been so certain that she'd join him in saving the Charrl; although how the bar in the safety-deposit box could help was beyond her.

Above her the grating moved.

'Bloody hell, it's like lifting a lead weight!' came a familiar voice.

Charlie?

The street urchin's face popped over the edge of the hole he had just uncovered. 'Cor, Benny, you're in a right pickle there, and no mistake!'

Benny tried to loosen the gag around her mouth and speak to him.

'Hang on,' he said, 'I'm comin' on down . . . '

A rope was lowered down, and Charlie shimmied down it. He took the gag out of Benny's mouth, and produced a knife with which he started gnawing at the rope. 'Bloody hell, it's like cutting through iron!' he said.

'That's because it's not rope – it's like the stuff insects produce from their silk glands.'

'That insect thing – it ain't going to come back then, is it?' he asked nervously.

'Don't worry, Charlie,' she reassured him and shook herself free of the constraints.

'Are you sure you can climb up this rope?' asked Charlie doubtfully. Benny wasn't like any woman he'd ever met before, but she dressed like a lady, and he couldn't quite imagine any English gentlewoman climbing up a dirty rope.

'Of course I can, Charlie,' she replied, and Charlie stood agog as Benny ripped off the lower half of her dress and stood there in front of him in a pair of silk bloomers.

'Well, don't just stand there gawping,' she said, 'give a lady a bunk-up!' Benny clambered up the rope as though she had been doing it all her life. As soon as she had reached the surface Charlie climbed up after her.

'Misha!' exclaimed Benny and planted a kiss on his cheek. 'You're always around when I need you!'

'I was at your lodgings in Dean Street sorting out Miss Waterfield's final effects when young Charlie found me and alerted me to your plight,' he explained and then noticed Benny's state of undress. 'Those scoundrels! They didn't . . . '

'No, Misha, they didn't,' she said, as the Russian hastily offered her his greatcoat to cover her state of semi-*déshabillée*. 'But thanks for caring anyway.'

'We must bring these villains to justice at once!' Popov declared melodramatically.

'Can we get home first?' she suggested. 'I now know what they want. I have to think what to do.'

'But tomorrow morning we contact the police, and charge this nefarious creature with kidnapping,' Popov continued. 'We have witnesses now!'

Benny raised a hand to her forehead – it was red hot and her bones were aching. *This is simply great,* she thought to herself. *I'm inoculated against every plague known to man, except the one which was finally eradicated in the 24th century.*

'Misha,' she said gloomily, 'just how many people died in the flu epidemic of 1918?'

'1918?'

'Never mind. Just get us a cab. I feel dreadful . . .'

'Hot water and whisky, that's what me mum makes for us when we have a cold.'

'Charlie, that sounds like a wonderful idea! C'mon, let's all go home!'

A few minutes after Popov had hailed a cab – the first motor car Charlie had ever ridden in – and travelled the short distance between Bloomsbury and Soho, Khan and Bellingham re-entered the empty cellar.

'She's escaped!' Bellingham gasped. 'But how?'

Khan sighed: Bellingham was a very stupid man, and what few brain cells he had left were now being eaten away by opium and syphilis. If not for his money and influence, Khan would have done away with his services years ago.

'I expected as much,' he said, as though he had planned her escape all along.

Bellingham looked curiously at his master: had Khan actually wanted Benny to set herself free?

'Then we must find her!' Bellingham panicked. 'If she tells the authorities . . . '

'Which she will.'

'She might dispose of the box – and then all our plans will have been in vain,' he snivelled.

'She will give the Charrl the birthright,' Khan said calmly. 'Did you not see her fever? She was attacked the other night. She has become infected by the Charrl.'

'How can you know that?'

'Our minds linked,' he said, ignoring Bellingham's gasp of

disbelief, 'and I felt the blood of the Charrl racing through her veins. Soon her allegiance to the Hive and its survival will be the only things in this life she cares about.'

'How can you be sure?'

'Because I am Jared Khan,' he said simply, 'and I have lived a long life, and learnt many secrets.' He reached into his jacket pocket, and took out a card.

'I drew the cards earlier,' he said, and turned the card over. he knew that this would impress the superstitious aristocrat, even though Khan had long since realized that predicting future events by the turn of the Tarot cards was, as Benny would put it, 'mystical twaddle'.

'The Ace of Wands,' breathed Bellingham and then smiled at Khan.

'Precisely. The Wand is now within our grasp, and the Great Divide will soon be open,' he enthused. 'Soon the birthright of the Charrl will be assured, and our glorious New Dawn accorded their just rewards.'

And it is indeed an enormous pity that when that does happen I shall not be around to see it, thought Khan, and smiled inwardly to himself.

Chapter 12

Schmidt's Wine House, 48 Dean Street, Soho, London, 2.30 p.m., Friday 23 April AD 1909

'In Russia this would not happen,' insisted Popov, as he slurped back a glass of Beaujolais in Benny's local. 'In the Motherland the police would listen and investigate our accusations!'

'In Russia they probably aren't in the pay of Khan and his cronies,' said Benny, who together with Popov had spent an unsuccessful morning trying to file an official complaint against Khan. 'Every single figure of authority in this blasted country seems to be connected with the New Dawn in some way or other.'

'The society has a long and influential history,' said Khan. 'Some say it is almost as ancient as the Knights Templar themselves.'

'And its base is in London?'

'No one knows. Some say London, some say Rome. At one time it was thought to have had its origins in China; people have even said that it truly began in Scotland some seven hundred years ago.'

'But I can't believe that all their members want the Charrl to overrun the planet,' said Benny, and sipped her wine thoughtfully. 'The Charrl would destroy them. Every species looks after its own kind first; survival is the paramount instinct . . . '

'Perhaps Khan has them all in his thrall?'

'It's possible. He has enormous mental powers – I've experienced them. I suppose it's just possible that he's placed them under some sort of massive hypnotic spell. After all, it can be done: just look at Hitler.'

'Who?'

'Never mind.' A worrying thought suddenly struck her. 'I once heard my friend, the Doctor, speak to me of a man he once knew. Called himself the Master. Master of what he would never tell me, but he was supposed to be one of the greatest mind-manipulators alive.'

'And you think that Khan might be this scoundrel?'

'Khan doesn't look anything like him,' Benny admitted, 'but he could have . . . disguised himself,' she said, choosing her words carefully so as to avoid discussing with Popov the finer points of bodily regeneration. 'But it's probably all a massive con job. The quest for survival might be a species' first overriding instinct, but it's closely followed by another one – greed. Look at Bellingham: he can't wait to get his little fingers on a bit of promised power.' She turned back to the matter in hand. 'So the police won't help us. What about Asquith?'

Popov shrugged his shoulders. 'I telephoned 10 Downing Street this morning, Benny. The Prime Minister's private secretary and MP for Mummerset West, Mr Edwin Rutherford, informed me that Mr Asquith is on a trip abroad.'

'Great! So that leaves only one option open for us.'

'And that is . . . '

'If no one is willing to believe us, then we'll have to bring them some proof.' She drained her glass, and stood up, slapping Popov amiably on the back.

'Tonight, Misha, you and I are going Charrl-hunting!'

As she climbed the stairs to her flat, Benny felt a stabbing pain in her side. Although the graze she had received from the Charrl had quickly healed itself, the skin which it had punctured still throbbed. Her headaches were getting worse too, and she longed for a decent aspirin.

She stopped at the top of the stairs. The door to the flat had been prised open. From inside the flat she could hear the rustle of papers, as the intruder searched through Margaret and Benny's papers, and some deep muttered curses. The burglar pulled open a drawer, and rifled through its contents, angrily tossing it to the ground when it was revealed that it contained nothing of interest.

'Nothing, sodding nothing! Where is it?'

At last some answers! thought Benny, and silently crept up on the mysterious intruder. But some sixth sense alerted the intruder to her presence, and a fist smashed out at Benny, hitting her in the jaw.

With a cry of pain – and a gasp of utter surprise – Benny fell to the floor.

Part Two

ACE

The planet Antýkhon in the year 2497 of the Great Migration

[illegible]

[illegible]

[illegible]

[illegible] There were about
[illegible] travellers
[illegible] and fresh water.
[illegible] which
[illegible] planet lived. She
[illegible] Heaven;
[illegible] and chose
[illegible] to stop travelling they
[illegible] Chief.

Most [illegible] sleeping bags, or

Chapter 13

Ace groaned, and rubbed more cream into the reddened skin of her face and her legs, as she had done every day for the past two months, ever since she had woken up and found herself mysteriously stranded on this goddamned planet.

She squinted up through the dark reflective glasses she always wore now, up at the scorching sun in the cloudless sky. Its ultraviolet rays were too much for her pale flesh, and it was only by a regular application of hi-protection block, orginally designed for colonizers of two-sun worlds, that she was able to save herself from skin cancer.

The morning's first and most important task completed, she went down to the stream to freshen up: the water tasted bitter and dead, but at least it wasn't poisonous.

Yet, she thought pessimistically.

She looked up in the distance, beyond the few barren and straggly trees and at the enormous pyramid shape of the Hive Imperial perched on top of the white cliffs overlooking the sea.

She was convinced that the effluent produced by the Hive had killed the river; a faint tang of ammonia hung in the air, and everyone knew that that was the stink of the body juices of the blasted Charrl.

She looked surreptitiously about the camp. There were about thirty people in this camp, of different ages and sexes, travellers who roamed the country in search of food and fresh water.

Many of them had escaped from the Shantytowns in which most of the inhabitants of this hell-pit of a planet lived. She thought fondly of Jan and his band of travellers back on Heaven: these travellers were different. Jan and the others had chosen their way of life; if these people chose to stop travelling they would die, prey to the Charrl.

Most people were still zipped up into their sleeping bags, or huddled in their skins around the remains of the campfire, around which two mangy dogs poked their noses.

Ace envied them the fact that they could sleep out in the open, and not in the tent which she had been forced to set up for herself.

Her friends called themselves Hairies, on account of the hair which covered a large portion of their bodies (even, to a certain degree, the women) and which also protected them from the more harmful ultraviolet rays of the sun. If not for her protective one-piece combat suit Ace would have been charred to a crisp long ago. She hardly ever took it off now. The fact that she probably stank to high heaven didn't really bother her; all the other Hairies did as well.

Satisfied that no one was up and about yet, she stole out of the camp to a small clearing, where she hurriedly tapped out a seven-digit code on the mini-computer which she wore on a gauntlet on her wrist. Quickly it interfaced with the radio communicator she always kept around her neck.

Ace listened, looking up hopefully into the early-morning sky. Nothing. Not even the monotonous pulse of a space beacon. All she could hear was a continuous buzz of static. Less excitement than good old Perivale on a Saturday afternoon, she thought glumly; at least there you could listen to Capital and see how Charlton Athletic were doing.

Whichever planet she had landed on must be so far out of the space lanes as to be insignificant. Her communicator could pick up on a sub-space frequency from a distance of 2.34 light years, or even more, depending on the level of technology of the sender. Even in the Outer Wastes she'd heard that Draconian satellites usually kept an ear open for signals of any intelligent life. The armpit of the Universe, that's where she'd landed.

She looked back at the Hive on the cliffs. No radio emissions from there either, which was hardly surprising. The 'science' of the Charrl was an organic and psychic one, and they never relied on conventional technology.

That worried Ace: she liked technology, felt comfortable around it, had proved she could handle it. Three years of dirty skirmishing for various Corporations and then in Spacefleet's Irregular Auxiliaries had taught her that machines don't let you down; well mostly they didn't, and when they did they could easily be reprogrammed or junked.

She punched out another code on her computer gauntlet, sending out a sub-etheric message to anyone who might be around to pick it up.

Like throwing a bottle into the bloody ocean at Kandalinga! she thought. *Don't hold your breath waiting. Christ, I have to get off this planet!*

A sixth sense told her she was being watched, and she quickly closed down the computer–communicator link, and spun around. Seeba was watching her slyly through narrowed eyes.

'Talking to your secret friends again, Ace?' he said suspiciously.

'There's no one to talk to, old mate,' she said bitterly, and regarded the bearded and burly man. 'Not another sodding soul for light years.'

'I told you before, we're off the space lanes. We've been a closed world for centuries,' he said. 'Who in their right minds would want to share this planet with the likes of the Charrl?'

Ace glanced over at the Hive on the clifftop. 'Is this the one then?'

'Must be,' Seeba said. 'There's not another hive around for miles. That's where my brother, Chel, was taken.'

'Then when do we attack?'

'You're the boss now, remember,' he said darkly. 'You decide.'

Ace glared at the forty-year-old guerilla: she knew what he felt towards her. Seeba had been the leader of his small group of Mammals scavenging the dead countryside looking for food and occasionally attacking patrols of Charrl until Ace had arrived.

After she had been accepted into their group, she had saved them all from a raiding party of Charrl, who were scouring the country looking for fresh mammal-meat to feed their grubs. For some reason, the human body provided a much better source of protein for the Charrl than the cattle which still occasionally grazed on hillsides where the grass had not been scorched away by the heat of the sun. Ace also suspected that the Charrl ingested humans' limited psychic abilities along with the protein.

The weak Charrl, unused to armed resistance, had proved no match for Ace's superior technology, and Ace had been voted in as their leader, replacing Seeba. She had protested that anyone with the right weaponry could have done what she'd done. But Ace was a fighting female, and as such considered superior to a fighting male. She had begrudgingly accepted the position, earning at the same time Seeba's constant hostility.

'Tell me, Ace, what's in it for you?' asked Seeba. 'You don't care less that Chel was taken from Shantytown, into the Charrl's larder. Why are you helping us?'

'The more Mammals that are free, and out of the Shantytowns, the more there are to fight the Charrl,' she said simply. 'Isn't that good enough for you, Seeba?'

'And what do we do then?' he asked pertinently.

'Turn yourself into an organized opposition and you'll be able to carve out enclaves for yourself; maybe even eventually determine your own existence. Prove to the Charrl that you're not going to stand meekly by while they cull you.'

'You know, Boss, we still know so little about you,' Seeba said. 'We know you're a fighter, and a killer. A good one, at that, although I've seen cleaner, more detached ones: you enjoy it too much. But you've got spirit. That's unusual round here: most of us are happy to be warded into Shantytowns, where the Charrl pick us off as and when they need. But we still don't know where you really come from – or what you really want.'

'I told you,' Ace replied steelily. 'I'm a fighter pilot. My spaceship crashed and I was stranded here.'

'We never did find the wreckage of your craft,' he reminded her.

'Don't you think I don't know it!' she snapped, her mind instantly going back to that point two months ago when she had arrived on this planet.

Seeba had hit on a sore point: she hated being out of control like this. That's why she had been eager to take over the command of Seeba's group.

'Now, come on!' she barked. 'We're wasting valuable time. Let's get back to the others.'

Interlude

The Planet Antýkhon, two months earlier

Ace awoke and raised her hand to her aching forehead; she had the mother of all hangovers. The ground on which she was lying burned her cheeks, and she felt the blazing heat of the sun on her bare arms.

Just let me lie here and die, she thought to herself. *I haven't felt this ill since I was a kid, drinking Southern Comfort underage in the clubs up West . . .*

Her Spacefleet experience reasserted itself, and she snapped out of her self-pity. She checked first that her wrist computer and sidearms were still there, and secondly that she hadn't sustained any injuries. Satisfied that everything, apart from the state of her head, was in order, she sat up, prised open two heavy eyelids, and looked around her.

A red sun blazed down from an almost cloudless sky, and in the distance bare brown hills undulated into the distance. It was deadly silent: not even a bird wheeled in the sky, and the rocky soil was dead and barren, without even an insect or worm burrowing into its blackness.

She stood up on shaking legs, and leant against the wooden exterior of the TARDIS, frowning as she tried to remember how she had come to be outside the time machine.

The last thing she knew she had been getting herself lost in one of the TARDIS's corridors. And that was weird for a start. Normally she had a perfect sense of direction, even in the constantly shifting and changing environment of the time machine.

This time, she had the nagging feeling that the TARDIS was playing a game with her, guiding her not to her room, but to where the ship itself wanted her to go.

The TARDIS's outside was warm to the touch as it reflected the heat of the sun. Ace wondered how long she had been unconscious; her arms were already blistered from the ultraviolet rays, and she reached into the weapons pouch which hung on her belt and fished out some sun protection cream.

'OK, Doctor, let me back in!' she shouted impatiently after she had smeared the cream into her bare skin.

She rapped sharply at the TARDIS's closed doors. There was no reply. 'Doctor? Benny?'

She knocked again, and one of the double doors creaked open.

Creaked?

She frowned and entered the time machine.

And felt very foolish as she realized she was standing inside a police telephone box.

'Doctor?' she said, and suddenly thought just how ludicrous it was calling out his name inside the small wooden hut. It wasn't as though there was anywhere for him to hide, she giggled nervously.

A telephone rested on a small ledge built into the corner of the police box, and she lifted it up. Nothing. Well, what did she expect? A hotline to Gallifrey?

In the light of the sun streaming in through the windows she scanned each of the police box's four walls. It was as if the TARDIS that she'd known had never existed: one small and solitary roundel, at the foot of one of the walls, was the only clue that it had ever been anything more than a plain London Metropolitan police box circa 1960.

Angry, and feeling deserted, Ace stormed out of the police box and slammed the doors shut behind her with such a force that one of the window-panels shattered.

She remembered the Doctor giving Benny instructions in how to land the TARDIS. Well, 'Professor' Benny Summerfield might have been duped, but not her. Ace knew that what he had told her hadn't formed any part of the landing procedures she knew.

So the TARDIS had vanished.

So the Doctor had gone off on his own.

And dumped her.

For a moment she felt a twinge of regret: had the Doctor really abandoned her after all? Ever since she had returned to the ship after three years in the 25th century there'd been a tension between the two of them.

Sure, things had often been strained between them before but this time it was different. They'd both developed a healthy respect for each other, but it was a respect which had both of them circling each other like two wary tigers waiting for the other to make the first move.

The Doctor had said that he'd needed a change, a rest. Maybe the crafty old buzzard had thought that it was time to get rid of her so that he and Benny could go off careering around the cosmos on their own? Who knew what went on in that eternally conniving and calculating whirlpool of his that he had the gall to call his mind?

So she was stranded on an alien planet.

So tough shit.

This wouldn't be the first time she'd been alone on some distant world, and she'd survived before. Realizing that the TARDIS was about as useful to her now as a box of Kleenex to a Cyberman – or a sense of integrity to the Doctor – she stalked off towards the hills in search of civilization.

As she moved off, following the course of a small stream, she chose to ignore the faint whiff of ammonia which hung in the air.

If she had looked around she might have seen, standing on the crest of a hill in the distance, the fat little man and his insect-like companion who had been watching her for some time, ever since the TARDIS had blinked into existence on the planet Antýkhon.

'Who is she?' asked Ch'tizz.

Shading his eyes from the light of the sun, Muldwych continued to watch Ace depart. There was a curious expression on his face, as if he recognized her from somewhere else, but couldn't quite place where.

'Highly dangerous, I'd say,' he said, and smiled. 'Light *her* blue touch paper and it would be advisable to stand well back . . . '

He pointed down at the dark shape of the abandoned TARDIS, and the sunlight bounced off the blue Roman-style ring which he wore on his left hand.

'The woman is of no consequence to your plans, however,

ma'am,' he said. 'That is what we need!'

'You are certain?' rasped Ch'tizz.

'This is life: nothing is certain,' Muldwych replied tersely, even though he was finding it incredibly difficult to contain his excitement. 'But if my researches are correct, that blue box will help to stabilize the Great Divide; and then let the Swarming begin!'

'You do the Charrl a great service, Muldwych,' said the Queen. 'Because of you our great race will survive. We will leave this damnable planet.' There was a tone of relief in her voice as she continued: 'And these Mammals will be left in peace.'

'I know the Charrl find killing abhorrent,' admitted Muldwych. 'I realize how difficult it must be for you to slaughter them for food.'

'The Charrl must survive,' she said simply. 'If that requires the massacre of this planet's entire Mammal population then so be it. And you will be honoured as the man who helped us to do so.'

Muldwych's brow furrowed in concern, obviously not entirely happy at the honour. Nevertheless he said:

'It's my pleasure, Your Majesty, it's entirely my pleasure!'

Chapter 14

'What you are saying is crazy!' insisted Seeba as Ace gathered around the camp fire with ten or so other members of their party. 'We need to attack in force if we are to get past the Hive's defences.'

'Perhaps Seeba is right, Ace,' said Marla, a young woman a few years younger than Ace, whose gentle nature and steadfastness had earned her the affectionate title of 'Mother' of the community. 'The Charrl are weak: a massive attack could do them a great deal of damage.'

'We're ten fighting people at the very most,' Ace pointed out. 'I'm not going in for any senseless heroics. This is a secret raid, right? We're doing this to save Seeba's brother, Chel, from ending up on the Charrl's dinner plates, OK?'

She glanced over at Seeba. She wondered if he knew that she couldn't care less about the life of his brother whom she had never met, but by saving his life she hoped that Seeba would owe her one: he was a good fighter and she needed him on her side.

Damn! This is what comes from travelling too long with the Doctor, she mentally scolded herself. *I'm getting as manipulative as he is*.

'The fewer of us who go in there, the sooner we'll all get out,' she said. 'I don't want any more deaths on my conscience than is strictly necessary.'

That shut Seeba up, but he still glowered moodily at her as, with a blackened twig, she made a sketch of the Hive in the dry earth.

Calling the Charrl's base a Hive was, she realized, in fact a misnomer. She remembered a trip with the Doctor to Africa a long time ago, and the termite mounds which lined the dirt-track road they'd travelled along.

That was what the Hive most resembled: a giant termite mound, even though this one stood about fifty metres high, making it about a third of the size of the Great Pyramid back on Earth.

'So what do you suggest, Ace?' asked Marla. A simple female, she would sway whichever way the wind was blowing. Ace was woman, so her words had more weight than Seeba's.

'How many Charrl do you reckon there are in the Hive?' asked Ace. The others looked at each other and shrugged.

'About four or five thousand?' suggested Skol, a grizzled middle-aged matter-of-fact man, whom Ace liked for his hardiness and simple approach to life, but mainly because he usually agreed with her. 'And their pupae of course.'

'If they're like insects back on Earth –' Ace began, and the others looked strangely at her. 'A planet a long way from here,' she explained quickly. 'But if they are like Earth insects there will be a hell of a lot more than a few thousand of them. A hundred thousand would be more like it.

'Now with that many of them down there the heat in there is going to be incredible. Together with that stink of ammonia, there's hardly going to be any oxygen in there at all.'

'So how do we get in there?' sneered Seeba. 'I suppose you just happen to have oxygen masks for all of us?'

'Don't be a dunghead, dunghead,' Ace riposted. 'The Charrl need oxygen as much as we do.'

'So how do they survive in their Hive?' asked Marla.

'Easy!' said Ace, and recalled the lecture a Masai chieftain had once given her and the Doctor as they stood by a termite mound in the Great Rift Valley.

('You should listen to this, Ace,' the Professor had said. 'You never know when it might come in handy.')

'They build thousands of tiny tunnels leading from the centre up to the surface of the nest. That way, the hot oxygen-poor air rises from inside the nest, to be replaced by the much cooler air from outside. A circulation of fresh air is created throughout the Hive.'

'I'm impressed,' Skol said. 'You're an intelligent woman, Ace.'

Marla, who wasn't particularly intelligent, was also impressed, but still couldn't quite grasp Ace's plan. 'What exactly are you proposing we do then?'

Ace grinned. 'We enter the Hive through the ventilation tunnels. Hey, I know it's corny: I've seen all those movies where the hero escapes through the ventilation system.'

'But won't there be Charrl in the tunnels as well?' asked Skol.

Ace shook her head. 'Not if they're like the termite mounds we have on Earth. If the Charrl inhabited the ventilation shafts it would defeat the whole object of the tunnels.'

'So when do we go?'

Ace glanced up at the sky. 'Just after noon, when the sun's the hottest. They'll be drowsy then. Skol, you come with me,' she said, and opened up her weapons pouch, taking out two small pistols which she gave to him and Seeba.

'What's this?' he asked.

'A blaster.'

'A weapon?'

'That's right. Standard Spacefleet issue. Much more effective than the bows and arrows and muskets that you lot use. It shoots a concentrated beam of plasma, enough to blast a careless Dalek all the way back to New Skaro.'

'Dalek?'

'Boy, are you lot ever a long way from the main space lanes.'

'You should know, Ace,' Seeba said darkly. 'As you travelled here in your ship.'

'Yeah, that's right, I did. Seeba, you'll come with us as well. It's your brother we're rescuing, after all. The least you can do is identify him.'

Two hours later the sun was at its zenith, and the heat was almost unbearable. Ace passed around rehydrating tablets from her weapons pouch; without them they would never survive the long journey to the Hive.

She squinted up at the sky. Unlike on Earth there were hardly any clouds in this planet's sky to offer protection from the sun's rays.

I wouldn't be at all surprised if the ozone layer hasn't been buggered up as well, she thought grimly. *The Charrl really screwed up when they chose this place for colonization. It's going to take some serious terra-forming before it's made even half-way habitable again.*

Rather than approach the Hive head-on, Ace had opted to go to the foot of the cliffs on top of which the Hive was built. There they would scale the cliff walls, hopefully avoiding any Charrl guards which might be watching over the shallow sea the Hive overlooked.

It was a plan which Seeba (predictably) opposed, arguing that they would never survive the longer journey, even with Ace's rehydrating tablets. But a threatening gesture of Skol's blaster, and Ace's argument that it was much better entering by the back door than risk coming across a party of Charrl scouts heading for the nearest Shantytown in seach of fresh meat, convinced him. Grudgingly Seeba agreed, and followed Ace and Skol off to the coast.

As they reached the pebbled beach, Ace looked out to sea. The ocean seemed unnatural: it was calm and still, undisturbed by any wind, and the squawks of the seagulls as they wheeled and gyred in the breeze; that sound that she always associated with the sea was noticeable only by its absence.

A dead sea on a dead world, she thought and shuddered.

Once when she had been a teenager Ace had loved the unfathomable mystery and unpredictability of the sea, and the sound of its waves lapping on sandy beaches; now she preferred the harsher blackness and colder silence of deep space. Three years of commando activity did that to a girl.

Skol and Seeba looked up at the white cliffs, and the base of the Hive, about fifty metres above them. It seemed an awfully long way to climb in this heat.

'Then the sooner we start the better,' Ace said, and hammered a spike into the base of the cliff wall. 'Watch out, boys,' she said. 'It's chalk and limestone.'

Slowly the trio made their way up the face of the cliff.

At the halfway point in their ascent, Ace stopped to allow Skol and Seeba to catch up with her and turned to look again at the sea. As she looked out over the water, she raised a hand to her glare-resistant glasses and activated a touch-sensitive control.

The focusing in her glasses responded instantly to the

command and adjusted itself automatically, offering her a magnified, if not quite telescopic, view of the horizon. It had been her own invention, and it had only taken some mild persuading on her part to get the Professor to make the adjustment to her sunglasses.

Far off in the distance she could just make out a hazy blue coastline. She frowned. For some reason it seemed familiar.

Don't be such a bilgebrain! she reproved herself. *Three years with the Professor and three more with Spacefleet and you're acting like a bloody tour guide to the Milky Way!*

With a grunt, she turned herself to the matter in hand and pulled herself up to the top of the cliff. Skol and Seeba soon followed her and all three gazed up at the Hive.

Close up it seemed enormous and was made of sun-baked mud and earth. At intervals of every few metres there were tunnels letting out the hot, bad air and letting in the fresh oxygen. Ace had been right: they weren't guarded.

'Now what?' asked Seeba.

'Now we go down into the larder!'

Interlude

In a chamber near the centre of the Hive nine Charrl sat in a circle around an enormous opaque ball. They were motionless, as they had been for hundreds of years, and the only evidence of any life at all was the sight of their antennae as they gently twitched in response to the Mammal-stench of Muldwych, who regarded them anxiously with the Queen.

Occasionally worker-Charrl, at five feet much smaller than the seated Charrl, would enter their chamber, bringing food for the nine.

'How fares the link with Earth, Muldwych?' Ch'tizz demanded of the Mammal.

Muldwych shook his head. 'Badly, I'm afraid, Your Majesty,' he admitted. 'The globe is serving as a focus for their psychic powers, but they are weakening steadily. Soon the Great Divide will close forever.'

'But we must cross our people over the trans-dimensional link to Earth,' insisted Ch'tizz. 'It is a young world, unsullied and verdant, a perfect world for the Charrl. Cannot you join your mind to the Chronomancers' and boost the power?'

Muldwych shook his head forcibly. 'My psychic abilities are weak compared to those of the Chronomancers, my Mammal brain unable to withstand the psychic trauma.'

Or just unwilling? thought Ch'tizz suspiciously.

'Only the Charrl have the required mental energies to stabilize the Great Divide, Your Majesty,' Muldwych insisted.

'But we are weakening, Muldwych. And the temporal energy released by the Chronomancers is sapping our strength even more. The Charrl we send over now can only remain on the planet for a few minutes before their bodies disintegrate, torn apart by the forces in the Vortex. Without the Great Divide stabilized we are all doomed. There must be something you can do!'

Muldwych sadly shook his head. 'In my youth I taught the Chronomancers to read the Time Lines, and to communicate telepathically across the Great Divide. But even I cannot breach it forever. Only one thing can stabilize the energies released on Earth, and open a permanent bridge between this world and that.'

'A wooden box!' scoffed the Queen, and indicated the police-box shell of the TARDIS which she and Muldwych had brought into the Hive two months ago when Ace had arrived on Antýkhon. It stood battered, and almost forgotten, in the neighbouring chamber. 'Better a court magician with his box of tricks than this half-crazed notion of yours!'

Muldwych ignored the Queen's scorn and sighed, as much with nostalgia as with puzzlement.

'Ah, but once upon a time that box was more, much more than a mere box. Why has it changed? Why?'

Chapter 15

Despite their function as ventilation ducts, the tunnels were filled with air that was still stifling and heavy, laced as always with the ubiquitous smell of ammonia. Ace, Seeba and Skol found it hard to breathe as they slowly edged their way down the inclined tunnel, grabbing hold of whatever handholds they could find in the crumbling tunnel walls as they made their descent.

After what seemed hours, but had been little more than twenty minutes, Ace's feet touched solid ground. She slipped herself out of the tunnel and helped Skol and Seeba.

She looked around her. The outside of the Hive was ugly and fortress-like, built for no other purpose than to withstand the ravages of this planet's climate. Inside, however . . .

Ace gasped.

They stood in a narrow corridor whose walls were covered with gossamer threads of gold and azure which twinkled and floated gently in the breeze from the tunnels. In the ceiling above them fluorescent stones had been set into elaborate mosaics, giving them not only light to see by, but, if they had examined them more closely, a pictorial history of the Charrl and their legends.

From somewhere far off came the tinkling of chimes, which were strangely musical and soporific in the warm air. Were it not for the still-pungent smell of ammonia, Ace would have believed that she'd landed in one of the famed pleasure palaces of Salostopus Four.

'Not bad,' Ace said approvingly. 'But how could anything so evil create something so beautiful?'

'I've heard some say that the Charrl are not evil in themselves,' said Skol.

'What d'you mean? Of course they're evil,' she protested. 'They take Hairies from the Shantytowns and use them as food!'

'We eat our cattle, Ace,' he pointed out. 'They've got to survive somehow.'

'On human meat? Don't give me that crap. They're just overgrown insects. And Earth insects get by, thank you very much, on plants, and flowers, and nectar –'

She stopped abruptly as she suddenly realized that, ever since she had been stranded on Antýkhon, she had not seen one flower or one green plant.

'Can you two stop apologizing for the feeding habits of our enemies,' interrupted Seeba. 'We came here to do a job!'

'Seeba's right,' said Ace. 'Let's worry about the morality of the Charrl later.'

'Where would the larder be?' asked Seeba.

'With the Queen,' said Ace.

'And where would she be?' asked Skol.

'Queens get all sorts of perks and little luxuries,' Ace reasoned. 'And what's the biggest luxury on this planet?'

'Water?'

'That's right. The larders will be at the very bottom of the Hive, nearest to sea level.'

'I was afraid you were going to say that!'

'Come on!' she urged.

'But which way?'

Ace pointed out to them that the floor of the passageway sloped downwards. 'All the chambers will have been built upwards from the central one,' she decided. 'So if we just keep on going downwards we're bound to reach it sooner or later.'

'Ace, you are exceptionally clever,' Skol repeated, as they made their way down the tunnel. Ace shook her head.

'I'm really as thick as a brick out-house; I only got two O-levels,' she admitted candidly, as she ran along the corridor. 'But I've got two things which are even better: a good teacher and a whole load of common sense! And there's something else I've learnt.'

'And what's that?'

'That the place you want to get to is always the place that is furthest away from a safe exit. Now let's get moving!'

As they raced down into the depths of the Hive Ace knew there was something wrong. If she had been right the Hive should have been teeming with thousands of Charrl. But as they ran through network after network of tunnels and honeycombs, they had to hide from very few. It was as if half of the Charrl race had disappeared – or died.

They darted into a large chamber near the centre of the Hive, and were suddenly confronted by a group of some twenty or so Charrl. Seeba whipped his gun out and was about to fire when Ace stopped him.

'Look at them!' she said.

The Charrl had noticed their presence, but seemed unwilling to do anything about it. Instead they gazed helplessly at the intruders and then chittered noisily past them, heading towards the surface.

'What's wrong with them?' Seeba whispered.

'They're dying,' said Skol. 'What's causing it? They must be even weaker than we thought . . .'

'Don't count your termites before they're metamorphosed,' cautioned Ace. 'The overriding concern of all insects is the safety of the Hive. That lot might be too weak to defend themselves, but there'll be plenty of warrior Charrl from where they came from.'

'Ace,' whispered Skol. 'Look here.'

He drew her attention to a sort of opening in the wall which looked down on a vast chamber. Within the chamber she could see nine Charrl seated around a glowing sphere, and outside the circle the tall figure of the Queen of the Hive and a plump little man.

'A Mammal?' Skol couldn't believe his eyes. 'A servant of the Charrl?'

'He's not a servant,' said Ace. 'Look at the way he's talking to her. He's an equal at the very least.'

Ace watched as the man spoke forcefully to the Queen, and then waddled over to a shadowy corner of the chamber, and showed something to her.

She bit her lip.

The TARDIS.

'Ace, I've found it!' cried Seeba, and pointed to a tunnel leading off from the main passageway.

In a massive chamber the size of a small church, countless

thousands of Charrl pupae were hanging from the ceiling, wriggling and twitching as they struggled to break free of their confines.

Slumped against the wall were hundreds of weak-faced Hairies, taken by the Charrl from the Shantytowns and drugged until the newly born Charrl emerged to devour them alive. Seeba rushed into the chamber, searching amongst the captured humans for his young brother.

'Seeba, come back!'

All pandemonium erupted. The pupae emitted a high-pitched chittering sound as they became instantly aware of the intruders' presence. Within seconds the nursery was full of warrior Charrl, alerted by the cries, and with the sole purpose of protecting the defenceless pupae who were the future of the Charrl race.

Using their enormous hind legs to propel them forward, they leapt onto Ace and Skol who blasted at them with their plasma guns. The first advance of Charrl fell back, to allow others to take their place, slashing at the two with razor-sharp claws and spitting burning acid at them.

'Seeba! Leave your brother!' Ace commanded, but he ignored her and continued to search through the captives for his brother. With a cry of triumph, he finally discovered him and dragged the dazed young man to his feet.

'You crazy sentimental fool!' Ace screeched, as she and Skol began to mow a path for them through the oncoming warriors.

And then, as soon as the warriors saw that Ace's party was leaving, they stood aside.

'What're they doing?' asked Seeba, who, along with Skol, was helping to carry his brother out of the nursery.

'Single-mindedness of purpose,' Ace said. 'They're leaving us alone, because we're no longer a threat to the nursery. But there'll be others – look!'

To their left a horde of screeching Charrl were pouring down the tunnel, falling over each other in their blind and instinctive compulsion to protect the Hive from its intruders. Like the sound of a million shrieking bats out of hell, their deafening squawking rang and reverberated throughout all the tunnels of the Hive, alerting their fellows to the danger.

Above the din Ace ordered Seeba and Skol to take the right-hand tunnel while she tried to hold them off with her plasma gun, whose power packs were beginning to show signs of needing to be recharged. She fired and fired and fired again, until the gun was hot in her hands, and still they came.

When she was sure that Seeba and Skol were clear, she ran off down the tunnel after them.

The tunnel was empty.

Behind her the Charrl were approaching. Frantically she dug her hand into the weapons pouch at her side, cursing the fact that she'd left her rucksack behind in the TARDIS – or whatever was left of it.

Then she was aware of a hand grasping her foot. Before she had time to resist she found herself being pulled down a tunnel, the narrow entrance of which was at ground level, like the opening to a pothole.

She landed with a bone-jarring *thunk!* at the bottom of the tunnel, as above her the screeching Charrl passed by.

'Ace? Are you safe?' she heard Skol's voice ask.

'The combat suit cushioned most of the impact,' she said and tried to look around. It was pitch-black.

'Where are we?' she whispered.

'Some sort of pothole,' Seeba said. 'Probably an old ventilation tunnel.'

'Hang on a second,' she said and activated the infra-red control on her glasses to enable her to see in the darkness. Skol and Seeba crouched before her. Seeba was cradling his stunned brother's head in his lap.

'You're right, it is part of a ventilation tunnel,' she said. 'But it doesn't go anywhere – it's a complete dead end.'

She scrambled over to examine the far wall. 'Look,' she said and drew their attention to the smooth face of the wall. 'They started digging and then had to stop – they couldn't cut through.'

'What is it? Rock?' asked Skol.

Ace adjusted the control on her blaster: this was going to call for some fine-tuning on the weapon. Otherwise the shock might bring the tunnel roof collapsing down on them. She aimed a steady beam of plasma waves at the wall.

'Remember I said this little toy could well and truly duff up a Dalek? Well, this stuff's a lot less tough than a Dalek's outer shell.'

'What is it?' asked Seeba.

'Concrete,' she said. 'Now get back to the far end of the tunnel – unless you want to be tonight's Ace-cooked dinner.'

Ace adjusted the control a fraction and a large chunk of concrete was blown out of the wall in a shock of dust and smoke. When the dirt had settled, Ace crawled through the hole.

A few minutes later her voice came back: 'Come on through . . . We're safe.'

The hole blasted out by Ace led out into yet another tunnel, and as Seeba and Skol helped the wounded Chel through, Ace could see that this one was much much larger than the ventilation tunnel of the Charrl Hive. The technology to burrow this tunnel out of the earth had definitely been mechanical, she decided; even the Charrl with their powerful mandibles could never have constructed something this huge.

Ordering her companions to link hands Ace guided them down the rubble-strewn tunnel. As far as she could determine, both from her own innate sense of direction and the fact that the tunnel had now started to rise at a steep angle, they were heading inland, away from the Hive and the sea.

A nasty – and preposterous – suspicion sneaked into her mind and she ordered her party to halt.

'What is it now?' moaned Seeba.

'There's the remains of an iron ladder here, set in the wall,' she explained. 'I'm going to go up. Wait for me . . . '

As she climbed up one rusty rung at a time the ladder creaked under her weight, but seemed secure enough. After a climb of a couple of minutes she found a circular panel of flaking rust set in the wall.

Its artificial symmetry, and the bolts around its outer rim, were of a technology totally alien to that of the Charrl.

Ace nodded wisely to herself, and rubbed the dirt from a cracked fragment of metal protruding from the wall next to the hatch. She peered through the darkness at the writing on it.

Now she knew why the coastline across the sea, and the white cliffs on which the Charrl had built their Hive, looked so familiar. Long ago, she'd visited both places on school trips.

She read the partly obliterated words on the panel:

Inspection H
European Chann
Dov

Chapter 16

'Antýkhon is Earth,' Ace stated, when they had returned to the camp. 'The planet I was born on.'

'You were born here?' Marla found it hard to believe. 'But you're so different from us, Ace – taller, smoother . . . '

'That's because I was born a long time ago, you see,' she said awkwardly. *Come on, think! How did the Professor handle these so-you-want-to-know-where-we-really-come-from situations?*

Seeba narrowed his eyes. 'How long ago?'

Now I remember: he told everyone the truth and to hell with the consequences!

'Oh, probably about twenty thousand years ago,' she said nonchalantly. 'And don't tell me it's impossible because that's what I used to say . . . '

'She thinks we're fools!' Seeba spat out the words with contempt.

'This is Earth,' Ace insisted. 'Its ozone layer buggered up, most of mankind extinct, but still my home. Don't you think I don't recognize the French coastline and the White Cliffs of Dover?'

Skol ignored Seeba's protestations, and asked: 'But if you are telling the truth . . . '

'I've travelled through time,' she said, anticipating his question.

'Pathetic lies!' Seeba sneered. 'How can she be our leader when she treats us as imbeciles?'

'I believe her,' said a weak voice. All eyes turned to Seeba's brother, who had been listening to the conversation.

'Chel? How can you trust her?' asked Seeba.

'Because that's what the Charrl are trying to do. I heard them discuss their plans when I was a prisoner in the Hive. They want to go back into the past of this planet when it was still young and fertile . . . '

'Can they do that?' asked Ace urgently.

'Not without Muldwych's help.'

'Muldwych?'

'A Mammal, the one you say you saw with the Queen,' Chel explained. 'He's helped to increase their psychic abilities to such an extent that they can open what they call the Great Divide . . . '

Ace listened as Chel told her of the Charrl's schemes and considered the matter. She supposed it was possible, especially if the Charrl were making use of some sort of disturbance in the time–space continuum.

And the TARDIS's crashing on Antýkhon might have been exactly the sort of disturbance they needed. With the help of someone like Muldwych, they might just be able to manipulate time.

She wondered who Muldwych really was. Chel had said he was just another Mammal, one who helped the Charrl and made periodic visits to the Hive; but Ace suspected he was something more than a mere Mammal.

A Time Lord? That was possible, probable even: the Professor's race, for all their insistence on a policy of non-interference, seemed to make a habit of getting their hands as dirty as possible on as many different worlds.

Ace realized – somewhat guiltily – that she didn't really care who Muldwych was, why he was on Antýkhon, or what his motives were in helping the Charrl. All she knew was that he and his insect allies offered her the only hope so far of getting off this isolated and barren planet.

'We've got to get back to the Hive,' she determined.

Seeba stared at her as if she were mad. 'That's crazy!' he said. 'What for? The Hive will be waiting for us! We'd be running straight into their larder!'

'Ace says there are other Hairies in the Hive,' said the soft-hearted Marla.

'That's right,' said Ace, not without genuine feeling. 'We can't let them die in there.'

'Do you really care for them, Ace?' Seeba asked pointedly.

'Or do you just want to join your time-travelling friend Muldwych?'

'He's not my friend. And yes, I do care what happens to them,' she said truthfully.

'And what can we hope to gain if we do succeed?' Seeba asked.

'Isn't the saving of lives gain enough?' asked Marla.

'A strike on the Hive might prove to be just the turning point you need,' said Ace. 'If we can show that the Charrl aren't as invincible as they make out, then maybe other Hairies will join us. We could launch a counter-attack against them, end their dictatorship.'

Seeba turned away in disgust.

'Ace is right,' said Skol. 'We've been idle for too long, doing nothing while the Charrl take Hairies from Shantytown to keep their larders well stocked. All we've been concerned about is our own safety, and making sure that the Charrl take someone else, and not us. Maybe it's time to stop running now and make a stand. Ace saved your brother's life, Seeba. Perhaps you should take that as an example.'

Seeba looked at Chel's supine form and then back at Ace. 'She doesn't give a damn about us,' he accused. 'All she's worried about is finding a route back to her own time.' Ace looked uncomfortably away. 'That's right, isn't it? Looking after Number One, aren't we – Boss?'

Ace looked warily at Seeba; the man's eyes were wide with rage. 'I kept our community safe for years before you came. Maybe it's time I took over again.'

He leapt to his feet and whipped out of his pocket the tiny blaster Ace had given him for the attack on the Hive.

Ace's hand instinctively went down to the weapons pouch at her side, but Seeba was too quick for her. He fired a warning blast into the dirt by her side.

'What do you want, Seeba?' she asked evenly.

'I want you to go back to your friends in the Hive, and let us be.'

'I'm sorry. I can't do that.' Ace's voice was calm and commanding as she looked Seeba right in the eyes. 'You see, I don't give a shit what happens to a toerag like you. But I do care what happens to Marla and the others. And if I can help them make a stand against the Charrl, then I'm going to do it. I don't like dictators, you see, whether they're insects – or human.'

Like lightning, Ace shot out a leg, hitting Seeba's arm. The gun went flying from his grasp, and, before he could reach for it, Ace had leapt from her seated position and had thrown herself onto the older man, knocking him to the ground. They rolled around in the dirt, first one gaining the upper hand, then the other. Ace punched Seeba in the gut, scarcely winding him, and Seeba responded by a vicious blow to the jaw. The rest of the Hairies stood around ineffectually, watching the fight.

After they had been struggling for a few minutes Ace managed to roll herself on top of Seeba. She began pummelling his face. 'Put up or shut up, Seeba,' she growled, and smashed his head brutally to the ground. 'We don't want your kind around any more!' She smashed his head to the ground a second time.

Skol laid a restraining hand on Ace's shoulder and urged her to stop. Seeba's face was already bruised and battered; he'd had enough. Ace stood up and watched as the defeated Seeba slowly dragged himself to his feet. He cast a vicious look at Ace.

'I'll stay,' he growled. 'But you're wrong.' He looked over to Chel. 'What do you think, brother?'

Chel shook his head. 'Ace is right: we can fight the Charrl – and we have to save the prisoners in the Hive.'

Seeba growled and with one final hateful look at Ace stalked out of the clearing.

'I've made an enemy there,' Ace said to Marla. 'First I take his command, and now his brother . . . '

'You may also have started a minor revolution,' Marla added.

Ace grinned. 'It's my speciality, Marla, it's my speciality!'

Ace had inspired the community. By making just one attack on the Hive and rescuing Chel, they had discovered that the Charrl were not quite so invincible as they had once thought.

That, together with Ace's leadership and the fact that the Charrl in the Hive were not as numerous or as strong as they had imagined, made another successful attack a distinct possibility. As night drew on there was a feeling of excitement amongst the community.

Ace's plan was to attack the following day, once again at noon, and to enter the Hive through the service duct of the Channel Tunnel. She was taking stock of the contents of her weapons pouch – her own plasma gun, and two smaller ones, and one small canister of nitro-nine (*not much to strike at the heart of another Evil Empire with*, she thought gloomily) – when there was a commotion outside the clearing. Ace jumped to her feet and grabbed her blaster.

Skol came into view, and Ace breathed a sigh of relief. He had been on a foraging expedition earlier, and had been late returning. Accompanying him was a young dark-haired man whom she didn't recognize; and, tied up and being led along by the rope Skol used to lasso cattle, the last thing Ace could have expected. She recognized the distinctive smell of ammonia and saw a quivering, frightened Charrl!

'What the hell is going on?' she demanded.

'Caught these two down near the Hive,' said Skol, and introduced the young man as Korin. 'That thing was taking it to the Hive . . .'

The Charrl turned to Ace, and replied in a shrill piping voice, 'I have rescued him from the Hive,' she claimed. 'I have brought him – and myself – here, as a token of good faith.

'My name is Isk and I want to help you all.'

Chapter 17

As Skol, Chel and the others watched on suspiciously Ace listened to Isk's story, all the time keepng her blaster trained on her. Ace was taking no chances; she had already seen the potential of the Charrl's razor-sharp claws.

Isk had indeed rescued Korin from the Charrl's larder and had been intending to bring him to their camp before Skol had captured her. Ace listened with growing interest as Isk told her of the Charrl's plan to travel back in time and colonize 20th-century Earth, and of their need for the TARDIS to stabilize the Great Divide before it closed and ruined their scheme.

'But you can't just go back in time, and take over the Earth,' she protested. 'Mankind would never allow it!'

'Mankind would have no choice,' said Isk simply. 'The Charrl are the superior species. Thousands of years of culture and artistry must not be allowed to vanish. The Hive must not die; it must continue – at no matter what cost to other species.'

'That's horrible!' said Marla.

'No. It's survival,' said Isk.

'So why have you come here?' asked Ace.

'I said that the Hive must survive, at all costs,' she explained. 'But there must be another way. Killing and subjugation is not the Way of the Goddess. The Charrl respect Life in all its many forms.'

'You have a strange way of showing it,' Skol pointed out. 'We saw your larder.'

'We do only what is necessary to survive,' said Isk, 'and the nutrients in the soil are wasted, and plants refuse to grow. It was the Mammals' neglect of their own planet that brought about that state of affairs.'

'And it's the effluent of the Charrl which poisons the rivers,' he countered.

'Can we discuss the ecological state of this planet some other time, please?' Ace urged. 'Carry on, Isk.'

She lowered her blaster slightly: Ace considered herself a good judge of people – though admittedly her experience of overgrown grasshoppers was slightly limited – and felt that Isk was being genuine.

'As I said, we venerate all Life,' she continued. 'Neither Ch'tizz nor any others of the Charrl wish to enslave the Mammals of the twentieth century. I have risked my life in coming to you. Can you help us find another way?'

Ace looked thoughtfully up at the darkening sky; she knew there was no chance of contacting anyone out there. In whichever century she'd arrived Earth was light years off even the remotest space lines.

She remembered the Professor telling her that several times in its future history Earth would be isolated and forgotten before becoming once again a focal point for the entire galaxy. It was just her luck for the TARDIS to dump her in one of those times when the Earth was the intergalactic equivalent of a ghost town.

She could teach the Charrl the rudiments of spacecraft construction, she realized. But it would take them years to construct a liner capable of carrying even half of their population to another planet and, as Isk pointed out, the Charrl were dying fast; they would never survive such a long journey. That was, of course, if they could find the minerals needed to power the ship.

The Professor. He'd know what to do, wouldn't he? But he'd probably already have done it and would just be waiting for history to catch up with him.

A glimmer of an idea formed in Ace's mind. It was an idea which might just get the Charrl off Antýkhon, leaving it to the Hairies, and at the same time give her back her freedom.

She turned back to Isk. 'Let me get this straight then. You need the TARDIS – or what I suppose is the real TARDIS – to stabilize the Great Divide. Otherwise your people are stuck here, where they'll become extinct.'

'Our people here will perish,' admited Isk. 'But the Charrl will not completely die out . . . '

'What?'

'The Charrl on Antýkhon will indeed become extinct, but not

the Charrl already on Antýkhon as it was, on the planet which you call the Earth.'

Ace looked suspiciously at Isk. This was getting to sound as complicated as one of the Professor's more dark and dodgy schemes.

'But you told me that the Charrl are so weak that they can't survive the journey back in time while the Great Divide is so unstable?'

'That's true. The Charrl who do get through die within minutes. But in that time they can "infect" the Mammals there with their seed.'

'You mean have it off with them?' This was getting too much, even for Ace's gruesome imagination. 'Have sex with them – copulate?'

'No,' said Isk.

'Well, that's a relief then . . . '

'Charrl eggs can be injected into a Mammal's body. When the egg hatches the grub will have a ready supply of food on which to feed . . . '

Ace shuddered. She remembered the Professor once telling her of an alien race which could propagate itself in a similar way; he'd called them the Wirrn. She'd been clearly unimpressed, having just taken a day off to watch a showing of the director's cut of *Alien* at Ealing Cinema.

'But how do you know this?'

'The Charrl we have so far sent across the Divide were charged with the task of dissecting the Mammals they encountered and examining them. They found that the Mammals of that time, untainted by any exposure to radiation or plague, make the ideal host body.'

'That's barbaric!' said Korin.

'No, it's survival,' came the predictable response.

Ace knew she had to do something. Not just to rid Antýkhon of the Charrl, not just to protect those women back in the 20th century who were being impregnated by the Charrl; but to get herself off this flea-pit of a planet and back into space which was where she belonged.

'Right, I've got an idea,' she said. 'Isk, can you get me into the Hive?'

Chapter 18

'So. What does this Time Vector Generator look like?' asked Ace.

Ch'tizz chirruped which Ace took to be the imperial Charrl equivalent of *Don't ask me, matey, I ain't got a clue,* or something to that effect.

'Muldwych will know,' said Ch'tizz, annoyed at Ace's abrupt manner but realizing that too much was dependent on this female Mammal now to give voice to her displeasure. 'He is coming now.'

It had been a novel and frightening experience for Ace, Korin and (with Ace's reluctant agreement) Seeba to enter the Hive through the front door, as it were. Isk had guaranteed their safety and when Ace had asked what authority the small shy Charrl might have in the Hive Isk told her that she was a Princess, one of the daughters of Ch'tizz.

Noticing Ace's look of surprise Isk chirped with what Ace supposed to be amusement. She needn't be that impressed, she'd told her; at the last count Ch'tizz had over twelve hundred daughters.

Ace whistled with astonishment. 'She must get well tired, then . . . '

'The survival of the race is all that matters,' intoned Isk.

'Yeah, so you keep saying . . . '

As Isk led them down winding passageways and past honeycombed chambers of sleeping (or dying?) Charrl, she told them of the flower-forests and the honey-pools of the original Hive World, Alya.

Ace was impressed, and even felt some pity for the Charrl; she supposed landing up on the Earth was a bit like leaving a private Caribbean island and having to make do with a night out in Ramsgate after the pubs had shut.

Isk finally led her in to the central chamber of the Hive where she introduced her three Mammal friends to the Queen of the Hive who regarded the three Mammals with distaste and some suspicion. Muldwych entered the room, and Ace noticed instantly that he made no obeisance to the Queen of the Hive. *So I was right,* she thought. *He thinks he's superior to her . . .*

She also noticed Muldwych's ruddy complexion and guessed correctly that the fat little man had been drinking. He beamed at Ace and held out his hand for her to shake: his touch was curiously dry and lifeless. 'Delighted to meet you, Miss –?'

'Ace will do,' she said tersely. 'Now what's this about a Time Vector Generator?'

'Ah, Her Majesty has told you then?' he asked. 'Let me think. How can I describe it to you? It is nothing less than a Magic Wand, a talisman of great wonder and powers, capable of bringing together the What Once Was with the What Shall Be, and rooting them both in the great What Is –'

'Cut the crap,' Ace interrupted. 'What exactly does it do?'

Muldwych's face fell: it wasn't often that he had the opportunity to give voice to his poetical nature. At least the young woman could have been a little more indulgent to a tired old man.

He waddled over to the battered shape of the TARDIS in the corner, and patted it affectionately.

'This is the machine that brought you here?' he said.

'I imagined you already knew that.'

'A marvellous creation, capable of spanning the dimensions,' he enthused, and opened the doors. 'And now nothing but an empty old box. The Time Vector Generator, when reconnected to the box, will enable the . . . the –' Muldwych looked at the legend above the TARDIS's doors – 'the "police public call box" to become whole again, reuniting its exterior shell with its true interior which exists outside of time and space.'

'So I find the Time Vector Generator, plug it into the TARDIS and – shazam! – the Great Divide stops wobbling?'

Muldwych clapped his hands together. 'Perhaps I wouldn't have put it in those exact words, Miss Ace, but that is more or less what I meant.'

'And where's the TVG now?'

'In the twentieth century.'

'How did it get there?'

'The TARDIS brought it there.'

Ace looked over at the police box shell of the time-machine. 'But it's here . . . '

'It is a time-machine, after all, my dear. It has existed – and is existing – at innumerable different points in time. As, indeed, are you.'

It was a slightly disturbing thought but Muldwych was right of course: there was no reason for her not to be able to leave the TARDIS at one point in time and then to come across it again at another point in time somewhere in the past or the future.

Of course, that should also have meant that there would also be a TVG on Antýkhon; she could see that even Muldwych was disturbed by the fact that there very obviously wasn't one.

'Right, now here's the deal,' announced Ace. 'You allow me and Korin and Seeba to cross over the Great Divide –'

'You'll be destroyed,' insisted Ch'tizz. 'The Charrl who have crossed over never return.'

Muldwych said nothing, just continued watching Ace through appraising hooded eyes.

'The Charrl are on their last legs – they couldn't survive a trip down the M1 let alone a few thousand years,' she pointed out. 'I'm a fit and healthy human.'

In fact, Ace hadn't the slightest idea whether her body could survive the trauma of being sent back in time. She knew that the Professor had done it, but then he was a Time Lord, and he'd survived lots of things which all natural laws said he shouldn't have done. Lady Peinforte and her servant Richard Maynarde had also time-travelled unprotected when they tried to get their hands on the Silver Nemesis. Hell, she'd even done it once herself but had never known whether she wound up on Ice World unscathed by good luck or because of the machinations of Fenric.

When it came down to it she was going to have to rely on a hunch – and a deep desire to get back to some sort of civilization.

'We go back to the twentieth century, and locate the TVG

for you. That will stabilize the Divide. That's my guarantee to you that I'm not going to go back on my deal. Your part of the bargain is that you release the Hairies you have in your larder; and that you're not going to come over.'

Ch'tizz bowed her head affirmatively. 'That is what I have promised.'

'And how do I know you'll keep your promise?'

Ch'tizz's whole body chittered in indignation. 'I am the Queen of the Charrl! We do not break our word!'

'They won't cheat on you, Miss Ace,' said Muldwych. 'Even the thought of death or enslavement is abhorrent to them. If there's any other way out of their dilemma then they will take it.'

'OK. Once on Earth, I send out a distress signal. By 1909 Earth had been under deliberate extraterrestrial observation for about a hundred years –'

'Really? You seem remarkably well informed, Miss Ace . . . '

'I hacked into Spacefleet records,' she admitted cheerfully. 'At least three races classed as non-hostile had their beady little eyes on Earth since the beginning of the nineteenth century . . . With my communicator I should be able to flag someone down.'

'And then?' asked Ch'tizz.

'We transport help to you through the Great Divide. Of course, if the TARDIS is there then so's the Doctor – I think. He'll be able to help you much more than I can.'

'And how can we be sure that you will be able to find the wand?' asked Ch'tizz. 'Our agent on the Earth has so far had no success . . . '

This was news to Ace. 'Agent?'

Muldwych's drink-ruddied face coloured even more. 'We have been able to use the powers of the Great Divide to reach mentally back through time and obtain assistance –'

'The girl need not know of every twist and turn of our attempts to stay alive, Muldwych!' hissed Ch'tizz. 'It is enough that the noble Charrl have to rely on her help in the first place!'

Suit yourself, Queenie, thought Ace. *I'll see what I can do for you as soon as I arrive. But if you really want to know the God's honest truth the most important thing at the moment is getting back to my Earth.*

'So,' she said, and turned to Muldwych, 'how do me, Korin and Seeba get to Earth?'

'If you will follow me,' said Ch'tizz, and led the way out of the chamber. 'The Chronomancers are waiting for you. They have been gathering their mental energies for some hours now.'

As they left the chamber Ace fixed Muldwych with her most dazzling smile. Embarrassed, Muldwych said: 'You are doing a great thing, Miss Ace. The Charrl are the noblest race of creatures this Universe has ever known . . . '

'That's OK, Mullie,' she said flippantly. 'Species-saving is my speciality.' She continued to look hard at the fat little man, who began to feel even more uncomfortable under her gaze.

'What's your game then?' she demanded.

'Game? I don't quite understand . . . '

'I don't think you're that concerned whether the Charrl live or die at all,' she said, and Muldwych raised an eyebrow as if to ask: *Well? Can you truthfully say that you are?*

'When you have known the Charrl as long as I have then you will realize how great their loss would be.'

'Yeah, I'm sure I would. But a friend of mine once told me that everything – from the big old Universe itself, right down to the tiniest speelsnake – has its alloted space of time. And that when that time's up you shouldn't mourn its passing, or try to stop it ending, but accept it graciously and be grateful for the good or bad it brought into the world. That's what the Doctor thought: I bet you think the same too.'

Muldwych refused to answer, and Ace continued:

'I think you're using the Charrl for your own ends, just as the Doctor used me until I got wise to him. You know more than you're letting on, Mullie.'

'Such as, Miss Ace?'

'For one thing, you know what the TARDIS is although you pretend not to. For another, you understand at least the basics of time travel.'

'I am a most voracious reader, Miss Ace, and in my long life have learnt many things,' Muldwych prevaricated. 'I would be happy to show you around my library on Mount Kukūruk some time. And you aren't unfamiliar with time-travel theory either.'

'Ah, but I've travelled with the Doctor. Where did you pick up *your* knowledge, Mullie? Gallifrey?'

Muldwych frowned. 'Gallifrey? I really don't know what you're talking about, Miss Ace.'

'Shame,' said Ace, 'we could have swapped holiday snaps,' and joined Korin and Seeba in the adjoining chamber.

Chapter 19

Hanbury Street, London,
11.15 a.m., Friday 23 April AD 1909

'Bloody hell, I feel like I've been put through a mincing machine backwards and then been fed to the dog,' groaned Ace as she raised herself up on the cobblestone floor and felt the April rain on her cheeks. 'No wonder the Charrl take such a bashing when they're sent back.'

She stood up on wobbling legs and looked around her. By her side Korin and Seeba were just regaining consciousness. 'See, boys, I told you it'd be OK,' she said with a brightness she didn't feel.

'Where are we?' groaned Seeba.

Ace looked up at the street sign. 'Hanbury Street. That mean anything to you?'

Korin glowered at her: how could it when he hadn't even been born for another twenty thousand years?

'It was where Jack the Ripper did in one of his birds! We're in the East End! Wicked!'

'Ace, this is wonderful!' said Korin and felt the refreshing rain splash onto his face.

'Haven't you ever seen rain before?' she asked and then remembered: 'Of course, you haven't – no clouds. Well, welcome to London, Korin. You'll get soaked here!'

'The air feels so fresh.'

'Make the most of it while you can, sunshine, because it's not going to last much longer. Another fifty years or so and then –'

Suddenly there was a warning shout from Seeba, who pointed down the street. A police constable was standing on the street corner, gazing appreciatively down at Ace's lithe figure in its close-fitting combat uniform. It seemed as if he was debating whether to arrest her for gross indecency or just stand there and enjoy the show.

'Morning, all,' Ace said, and saluted. 'You want something or what?'

PC Reggie Hawkins blushed slightly and coughed. 'I was just wondering if those two ruffians were bothering you, ma'am.'

'Ruffians?' Ace said, and then realized he was talking about Korin and Seeba. Unshaven, and dressed in muddied and torn combat uniforms and animal skins, she supposed they did look suspicious.

'Nah, they're my mates, officer,' she said, and shimmied seductively up to the police constable, putting a friendly arm around his shoulder.

'If I may say so, miss, you're hardly dressed for this kind of weather,' Hawkins said, trying (unsuccessfully) to ignore Ace's taut firm thighs and her pert breasts. 'We're due for a storm tonight.'

He took off his cape and wrapped it around Ace's shoulders. 'There, miss, that should keep the chill off you nicely. You ought to be careful around here, too. I've received a call at the station that there's some villainy afoot here. Though where it might be I've haven't the slightest way of knowing.'

'Well, thank you kindly, sir,' Ace cooed and attempted a girlish curtsey. When she deliberately lost her balance, Constable Hawkins bent down to help her up.

'Ace, was that really necessary?' asked Korin as they turned the corner of the street.

'He was asking for it!' Ace insisted. 'Sizing me up like an old lech! He wasn't even my type!'

'It was a stupid thing to do!' Seeba said.

'I've only stunned him, bogbrain!' she said. 'In a couple of hours he'll wake up from that blast from my plasma gun with a cracking headache and nothing else.'

'It was still idiotic.'

Ace stopped and rounded fiercely on Seeba. 'Look, you're on sufferance here, OK? I'm the boss, remember?' she said. 'And how do you think we're going to get around London without this?'

From out of her weapons pouch, she drew out the wallet she'd lifted from the police constable's pocket. 'This isn't Antýkhon now, Sunny Jim, it's 1909, and you need dosh!'

Korin looked around at the bustle of people on Commercial Street, and the horse-drawn carriages and motor-powered omnibuses which thundered down the road. 'It's fantastic, Ace,' he marvelled. 'I never imagined there could be so many people.'

'You should see it when the yuppies and developers hit the place,' Ace said ominously.

'So where do we go from here?' asked Seeba.

Ace handed each of them several notes from the wallet. 'Ch'tizz says there are still three Charrl around here, ones who survived the journey across the Great Divide. They'll be waiting to plant their eggs in the nearest likely candidate . . . '

'So?'

'The East End is the crossing-over point between Earth and Antýkhon, or so Muldwych said,' she explained. 'They won't have moved far from here. Ask around the pubs and the shops. See if anything unusual has been happening in the past few days.'

'Like what?'

'You tell me!' she said, and shrugged. 'Strange illnesses? Mysterious disappearances? Muggings?'

'And what are you going to do?' Seeba asked.

'Find the TVG, what else?'

'And just where are you going to start looking?' Seeba sneered. 'This is a big city.'

'I was afraid you were going to ask that,' she said glumly.

In fact, she hadn't the faintest idea where to start looking. The Professor had once offered her a homing device which would always lead her back to the TARDIS. At the time she had refused it; now she wished she had accepted it.

Ace pulled out a dog-eared business card from the wallet, a business card which had been given to Hawkins on a dark and foggy night almost three months ago. That night he'd been in the Ten Bells pub all night with his two friends, that butcher and that Scottish bloke.

She read the address on the card: this was either an incredibly lucky break, or . . .

She remembered what she'd said to herself earlier: *The Doctor would know what to do, wouldn't he? But he'd probably already have done it and would just be waiting for history to catch up with him.*

'What about 39 Dean Street?' she said decisively.

'Where?'

'I'll see you there later,' she grinned, and waved the business card at them. 'I've got an appointment now – an appointment with a Doctor John Smith!'

'What's he done with it! Where the hell is he?' Ace asked herself as she looked helplessly around the chaos she had created in Margaret Waterfield's flat in Dean Street. It had been easy enough to break into, but now that she was here she could find nothing which might even give her a clue to the location of the TARDIS, let alone the Time Vector Generator itself.

She had pulled drawers out of their cupboards, strewing their contents onto the floor; ripped open newly repaired cushions in the hope of finding something hidden in them; she had even torn up the floorboards. But the only thing she could find that was of any vague interest was a pass book to a posh people's bank, and a wardrobe of piss-elegant dresses which she thought probably belonged to a very amateur production of *My Fair Lady*.

'Nothing! Sodding nothing!' she said and momentarily tensed, as she heard the creak of a floorboard behind her. Then her training reasserted itself, and she relaxed.

Don't let them know that you know, she remembered. *Pretend that there's nothing unusual, and then, when the second that their guard has dropped –*

Ace whirled round and struck out viciously at her attacker.

Part Three

BENNY AND ACE

London, Friday 23 April 1909

Part Three

[illegible]

[illegible] Benny [illegible]

[illegible]

and, when Benny turned to [illegible]

'[illegible]?'

[illegible] Benny [illegible]

[illegible]

Benny [illegible]. 'You've [illegible]?'

'Again? [illegible],' [illegible]. 'Again?' [illegible]

[illegible],' said Benny.

[illegible]

'Are you OK?' asked Ace, with genuine concern. 'I really [illegible]'

Benny [illegible]. 'I must be losing my touch,' she [illegible], and raised a hand to her forehead; her temperature [illegible]. Before I joined the Doctor I'd never have let someone take me by surprise like that.'

'Where is he then?'

'Who?'

'The Doctor, of course,' [illegible]. 'He must be around here somewhere.'

Benny regarded [illegible] suspiciously. 'I thought he was with

Chapter 20

39 Dean Street, 2.45 p.m.

'Benny?'

'Ace?' Benny shook herself conscious as Ace hurriedly reached down and lifted her up off the floor where she had knocked her down. Benny stumbled to her feet, while Ace regarded her early-20th-century clothes with wry amusement.

'Been dancin' all night then, have you, Eliza?' she sniggered, and, when Benny failed to understand the reference, added: 'Never mind. What gives, attacking me like that?'

'I thought you were a burglar,' Benny claimed.

Ace looked suspiciously at her. *Come on! Since when did 1909 burglars go around wearing one-piece combat suits like mine, with the name 'Ace' written on the back in big red letters?*

Benny looked around at the devastation of the flat. 'You've broken into the flat! Not again!'

'Again? What do you mean, ''again''? I've only been here a couple of hours!'

'Forget it,' said Benny.

Stop trying to blame others, she told herself. *Face up to the fact that it was Margaret who ransacked her own flat that first time. You can't keep blaming everything on Ace.*

'Are you OK?' asked Ace with genuine concern. 'I really landed you a whopper didn't I?'

Benny massaged her jaw. 'I must be losing my touch,' she said ruefully, and raised a hand to her forehead: her temperature was blazing now. 'Before I joined the Doctor I'd never have let someone take me by surprise like that . . . '

'Where is he then?'

'Who?'

'The Doctor, of course, stupid! He must be around here somewhere!'

Benny regarded Ace suspiciously. 'I thought he was with

you . . . '

'And I thought he was with you,' she said, and took the business card out of her weapons pouch, and handed it to Benny.

'Where did you get this?' she demanded.

Ace flushed with embarrassment and looked awkwardly down at her feet. 'From a copper, like. He should just be waking up by now,' she said, and told Benny the story of her encounter with Hawkins.

Benny grinned in spite of herself. 'A policeman who just happened to be carrying a business card with this address, who just happened to be passing by.'

It was a weird coincidence, Ace had to agree. 'I remember he said something about someone ringing him up to say there was a major riot or something going on.'

'And was there?'

'Nah. As quiet as a victory celebration at Millwall . . . .'

Benny might have guessed.

'The Doctor again. Or one of his friends. *Medicus ex machina.*'

'Huh?'

'It's Latin for an interfering old goat, Ace.'

'What do you mean?'

'Ever since I arrived here, the Doctor's been manipulating things,' said Benny. 'Leaving little clues, prodding me in some direction or other – and you as well by the sound of it. I feel like a pawn in a blasted chess game, Ace.'

'I know what you mean,' Ace sympathized. 'Trouble is, they keep changing the chess player.'

Benny indicated the ransacked room. 'What were you doing here, Ace?'

Ace rubbed her neck where Benny had tried to throttle her, and looked warily at her companion. 'Er, looking for some clue to the Professor's whereabouts,' she lied, as Benny went to clear up the mess. She picked up the Coutts pass book.

'Have you been looking through this?' she demanded sharply.

Like she's trying to hide something, thought Ace.

'You're a rich lady, Benny,' she said. 'Where did you get all the dosh from?'

'It's not mine, it's the Doctor's,' said Benny. 'Look, Ace,

it's nice to have you with me and all that –'

Oh yeah?

' – but just how did you get here?'

'Time storm, wasn't it?' she lied. She wasn't going to tell Benny too much until she knew exactly what was going on. Not that she didn't trust her companion but . . .

'The TARDIS must have blown a fuse or something. Blacked out; next thing I know I'm in the East End!'

'Something similar happened to me,' Benny said and started to tell Ace about the 'dead' TARDIS on the Thames. 'Wait a minute – did you say the East End?'

Ace nodded. 'Yeah. So?'

Benny smiled. 'Oh nothing at all, Ace,' she said, keeping her suspicions to herself. She moved in to the kitchen. 'Tea?'

'Sure, two lumps,' she said as she followed Benny into the kitchen. *And two TARDISes,* she realized.

Two TARDISes separating me and Benny by tens of thousands of years. Like the TARDIS wanted to keep us apart . . .

[illegible]

[illegible] New Dawn. And if he

Interlude

31½ Museum Street, Bloomsbury, 3.45 p.m.

'Khan? Khan, are you there?'

Lord Bellingham rattled the door which led to his leader's private apartment above the bookshop. There was no reply, and Bellingham had looked in the cellar too. Finally Bellingham assumed that Khan must have left the shop for a minute.

He shrugged his shoulders: his business with Khan wasn't that important anyway, and could wait. He left the shop, but not before opening the till and taking out a crisp five-pound note; Khan made so much money from his book-selling, and from donations given to him from members of the New Dawn, that he wouldn't miss it.

In fact Khan was well aware that Bellingham had been stealing from him for some months now, but chose not to confront the young aristocrat with the fact. It was enough that he knew, as he also knew of Bellingham's other criminal activities, and of the secret vices of numerous politicians, and of the dubious financial interests of two members of the British Royal Family; they were all weapons he could use against them when the time was right, and in the meantime they ensured continued loyalty to the New Dawn and himself.

Jared Khan indeed possessed great psychic powers, perhaps more than any other human being in the history of the world. As Benny had guessed he was also a master hypnotist, able to bend most people to his will with ease. But years of experience had taught him that the greatest way to make people do his bidding was not mind-manipulation, but simple, good old-fashioned blackmail.

Lying back in the easy chair in his study, Khan heard Bellingham leave. The man was an insidious and vile specimen, Khan realized, but he tolerated the young aristocrat for the money and influence he brought the New Dawn. And if he wanted to feather his own nest at the same time, well, as the youngest son of an earl with a large family and with no talent whatsoever Bellingham had to survive somehow.

Khan's apartment was his own *sanctum sanctorum*, which everyone was barred from entering. Indeed, no one other than Khan had ever entered it since the day he bought the freehold of the shop, over ten years ago. Here Khan allowed himself to drop the facade he presented to the rest of the world as the magus of the New Dawn, to become the person he really was.

In the easy chair sat an enormously tired old man, whose hooded eyes stared blankly into space, and whose spirit and energies, if no longer his limbs, had atrophied almost past redemption

All Jared Khan had left now was his knowledge, knowledge accumulated over many long and hurting years, and which still did not quench his burning thirst for more; and the hope that the thing for which he had quested for a lifetime would soon be his.

For Jared Khan had taken the bonny, bonny road, and now that pathway was nearing its end.

Chapter 21

4.30 p.m.

Ace put her hand to Benny's wrist and felt her pulse: it was racing wildly now, and her nightgown was soaked in sweat. Ace wondered whether she ought to call for a doctor, and then thought of the problematic questions that would provoke.

Benny would be all right, Ace decided; all she had was a small dose of the flu – and a medium dose of the knock-out drops Ace had surreptitiously slipped into her tea.

'Sorry, Benny,' Ace whispered – and surprised herself by meaning it. She bent down and carefully removed the keychain which hung around Benny's neck. The TARDIS key glinted in the light along with the key to Margaret's flat and the Coutts safety-deposit box, and Ace felt another twinge of regret, if not a sense of betrayal, that the Doctor had chosen to give the TARDIS key to Benny and not to her.

Don't kid yourself! she reprimanded herself. *He certainly didn't give her this key out of the goodness of his hearts. I'm beginning to think that he never does anything without at least two different – and usually conflicting – reasons.*

Ace threw on one of Benny's coats, not in any attempt to conceal her combat uniform from curious eyes, but simply because it had started to rain heavily outside, and, with a final guilty look at Benny on the bed, silently left the flat at 39 Dean Street.

6.30 p.m.

In a small secluded alleyway behind Coutts offices in the Strand, Ace tapped out a command on her wrist computer. 1830 local time, the LED informed her, also adding, with, she hoped, unintentional mechanical irony that there was an abnormal level of precipitation in the atmosphere.

Thanks for telling me something I already knew! she cursed, and pulled away her rain-soaked hair from her forehead. The rain was coming down in torrents now, flooding the narrow cobblestoned alleyway, and Ace was grateful for her protective high boots: without them, she realized, she'd be a prime candidate for a class-one case of pneumonia.

She looked up at the window at the corner of the building. *OK, I know this is 1909 and it's supposed to be the Empire the sun never sets on*, she thought, *but do people here never bloody go home?*

She'd been waiting outside in the rain now for almost two hours, and still the light from the director's office hadn't been extinguished.

6.40 p.m.

Jared Khan stared deep into the large crystal ball in the centre of the table. Around the table sat Bellingham, the MP Edwin Rutherford, and Matilda and Agatha, the two friends of Margaret Waterfield.

None of them realized that Khan had no need whatsoever of the crystal ball to act as a focus for his mental powers; but it impressed them, and inspired in them a sign of awe, and that was why Khan used it.

Khan's eyes shone brilliantly as he made contact across tens of thousands of years in time. Before his eyes – and his eyes alone – there appeared the shadowy form of Ch'tizz, Queen of the Hive Imperial, Stewardess of the Noble Race of the Charrl, and Khan's constant associate for as long as he could remember.

Khan's lips moved but no sound came from his lips.

'What is he saying?' piped up Agatha.

'Shut your mouth!' hissed Bellingham. 'He's made contact!'

Khan's mouth continued to open and close soundlessly. After about five minutes he snapped out of his trance.

'Did you – did you speak to Ch'tizz?' asked Rutherford.

Khan stood up from the table. 'I spoke to our spirit guide,' he said, and smiled. It amused him to couch his words in terms these superstitious peasants would understand. 'She says that our Holy Grail is near at hand. Soon the New Dawn will possess mystical powers beyond imagination. Soon we will be granted the power and influence to bring peace and order to an unco-ordinated and ever more chaotic world.'

Matilda clapped her hands with glee. 'How sad that Margaret can't be here to witness this!' she squeaked. 'She did so love peace and quiet!'

Rutherford looked earnestly at Khan. 'And this power will mean an end to man's trials, an end to all the suffering and starvations in the world?'

'Of course, Sir Edwin,' oozed Khan, 'And in the New Order the world will surely applaud your part in the great scheme of things.'

'It is only my duty,' said Rutherford. 'My Christian duty . . . '

Even though it means dealing with the devil himself? Khan asked himself.

Bellingham did not say a word, just dreamt of the influence he would wield, and the riches he would reap, when the world was re-organized the way he wanted it. Khan was an old man; once the spirit-power was released Khan was disposable, and every penny he'd poured into this enterprise would not have been in vain.

Khan turned to Agatha. 'Miss Winterbourne, perhaps you'd like to read the cards for us,' he suggested.

Agatha nodded eagerly and took a pack of Tarot cards from a drawer and spread them out face downwards on the table.

'Turn the first one over,' instructed Khan.

Agatha did as instructed. The card showed a beautiful youth dancing in the middle of a wreath.

'The World,' breathed Bellingham, impressed.

'The successful completion of all our endeavours,' said Khan. *The wheel has turned full circle, and soon all knowledge, all power will be mine!*

6.50 p.m.

About bloody time! thought Ace as the light in Malcolm's office was finally extinguished. She waited another ten minutes, until she was sure that the director had left the building, and then took her blaster out of her weapons pouch, and aimed a carefully regulated beam of plasma energy at the bolted back door.

Once inside the bank, she adjusted the infra-red control on her glasses and looked around the main banking hall. It was eerily silent, a stark contrast to the hustle and bustle which usually filled the hall during the day.

The lights suddenly came on.

Shit!

An elderly night watchman, dressed as elegantly as the bank's daytime employees, was standing in the doorway, a billy club held threateningly in his raised hand.

'All right, come on out quietly like, Miss . . . ' he began.

'Sorry, no time to chat,' said Ace and fired a blast of plasma energy at the night watchman who crumpled to the floor. Ace just hoped she'd set her blaster to stun; there was a time when she might have stopped to check, but that was three years ago. Now all that mattered was regaining the TVG; and at least with the watchman out cold there'd be no one to alert when she blew open the strongroom door.

The strongroom was down in the basement of the bank, one of the most secure places in the London of 1909. It took Ace less than a minute to break into it.

Good old nitro-nine, she thought with genuine affection as the smoke from her last remaining canister of the explosive settled. *Plasma guns, wrist computers, X-ray specs might all be really cool; but there's nothing more satisfying than a bloody good bang!*

She searched among the numbered drawers in the strongroom for the one bearing the Doctor's number which she'd remembered from the Coutts pass book in the Dean Street flat. Finally she located the one she wanted and with the help of another bolt of plasma energy 'unlocked' the drawer, and took out its contents.

Like Benny before her she recognized the superstrong alloy used in the box's construction. Not quite as impregnable as the casket which once contained the Hand of Omega, she granted, but impressive nonetheless.

She reached in her pouch for Benny's key, and remembered the Doctor's words when he had handed Benny the keys almost two months ago now: *It can only be used by you, Benny, or another member of the TARDIS crew.*

Ace shrugged philosophically. *Well, here's my big chance to find out if the Doctor still considers me a member of his crew, or just another prize pain in the arse he should have dumped with Fenric when he had the chance!*

She inserted the key into the specially constructed trimonic lock, and turned. A few long seconds passed, and then the lid of the box slowly lifted open.

Ace reached into the box and took out the long ebony Time Vector Generator. As she held it in her hands it began to tingle, as if it recognized Ace's touch, and streaks of golden light began to flutter and shine within its dark interior.

'Gotcha!' she breathed and carefully closed and replaced the Doctor's box. She left the strongroom and stalked out past the still unconscious night watchman.

Outside the rain was even heavier, and large brooding thunderclouds were brewing. With the TVG hidden under her coat, Ace made her way back to Soho.

7.45 p.m.

When Ace turned the corner into Dean Street, she saw two bedraggled characters banging loudly on the door of Number 39. She marched up to them.

'What d'you want?'

Popov turned to Ace, and doffed his hat. 'Miss Summerfield who lives here. My friend and I are most concerned –' he introduced Ace to Charlie who was standing next to him – 'we were due to meet her here tonight, but she seems not to be answering the door . . . '

'I'm a friend of Miss Summerfield,' Ace said. 'What do you want with her?'

'We're going Charrl-hunting,' Charlie said, before Popov could stop him. 'What's the matter?' he asked. 'She ain't going to know what they are!'

Ace took out her key and opened up the door. 'I think you two had better follow me upstairs . . . '

* * *

The atmosphere in the Hive was electric, and the chamber of the nine Chronomancers was crowded with scores of expectant Charrl. Ch'tizz had allowed them to enter; normally the Charrl were encouraged to keep their distance from their Queen, but Ch'tizz had realized that events had reached such a stage where all normal formalities could be suspended.

Ch'tizz had kept her promise to Ace. In the larders, bewildered Hairies were being freed and herded out of the Hive. Now Ch'tizz prayed to the Goddess that Ace would keep her part of the bargain.

She looked over at Muldwych, who had been staring into the central globe for over an hour now.

'Muldwych?'

The fat little man snapped out of his reverie. 'Forgive me, Your Majesty,' he said. 'I was just . . . remembering . . . '

'You know these Mammals better than I,' the Queen said anxiously. 'Will the female Mammal keep her promise?'

Muldwych nodded. 'Ace will stabilize the Great Divide,' he agreed. 'And send help . . . as long as you keep your part of the bargain, not to travel over to Earth.'

'We are Charrl,' declared Ch'tizz. 'We do not break our word.'

Muldwych frowned as the noble Ch'tizz turned away from him.

Guiltily?

'And then the race of the Charrl shall be free.'

'Yes, Your Majesty,' agreed Muldwych. 'At long last freedom.'

For both of us.

8.10 p.m.

Popov's first concern had been for Benny, who, Ace had maliciously assured him, was recovering from a particularly unpleasant hangover, the result of her bumping into Ace, her long-lost friend, a few hours earlier and having celebrated with a few too many bottles of brutal wine.

After Popov was satisfied that Benny would soon be fine and in the best of health again, and Ace had replaced the keychain around Benny's neck, he had told Ace about all the events leading up to her appearance in London.

As she hid away the TVG in a drawer she was particularly interested in hearing about Jared Khan, recognizing him as the Charrl agent on Earth, whom Ch'tizz had mentioned.

There was a knock at the door. Warily Ace opened it. Seeba and Korin were standing there, their faces ashen and tired.

'You've found the Charrl?'

Seeba nodded. 'And you're not going to like it . . . '

10.10 p.m.

Ace, Popov and Charlie stared down in horror at the three husks of the Charrl which Seeba and Korin had found in an old disused yard, just off the Commercial Road. The Charrl had been dead for at least a day, and their bodies stank of released ammonia.

'Looks like the trip across the Great Divide was too much for them in the end, after all,' she said, and cursed.

'So what are you so upset for?' asked Charlie. 'They're dead, ain't they? Ain't that what you want?'

Ace shook her head vigorously. 'I needed them alive, Charlie. Without them we'll never know which women they infected with their seed.'

'So, Miss Ace?' asked Popov. 'What will happen if we cannot trace these women down?'

'*Alien 4,* Popov, that's what . . . '

11.33 p.m.

As soon as they arrived back at the flat Popov went into the bedroom to reassure himself that Benny was feeling better. He rushed out.

'Miss Summerfield has gone!'

'Damn!' Ace went directly to the sideboard and ripped open the drawer. 'She's taken the TVG!'

'The what?' asked Charlie.

Popov was much more concerned with Benny's whereabouts

and shared his concern with Ace. 'The rain is coming down in dogs and cats,' the Russian said. 'Benny is ill; ever since she was attacked by that monstrosity in the alleyway –'

'Attacked?'

'She was attacked by a Charrl some days ago –'

'You idiot! Why didn't you tell me? She's been infected by the Charrl!'

'Infected?'

Ace was already making for the door. 'Come on!' she ordered. 'I know exactly where she's going to be!'

Chapter 22

The banks of the Thames, midnight

The rain slammed mercilessly down on the outside of the TARDIS where it stood on the riverbank, half-submerged now by the rising tide of the Thames. The wind whipped the waves even higher, and in the purple-dark sky thunder cracked and lighting forked.

On a small mudflat near the TARDIS Benny, dressed only in her nightgown and an old coat of Margaret's, was sitting, cradling the Time Vector Generator in her arms. Her clothes were soaked and covered with mud, and her dark hair was plastered against her skull. The TVG twinkled brightly in her hands, as if anticipating its reunion with the TARDIS and the police box's transformation once more into a time machine.

Benny, now almost completely under the spell of the Charrl, with the seed of the Charrl coursing through her veins, gazed with longing at the police box. She started to whimper as the small part of her consciousness that was still her own fought a losing battle with the group mind of the Charrl and their desperate quest for survival. Slowly she dragged herself to her feet, slipping on the mud, and stumbling over the detritus on the riverbank. She began to move towards the TARDIS.

'Benny!'

Benny looked up curiously, over at the Embankment, where Ace, Popov and Charlie, Korin and Seeba, were peering down at her. Benny frowned: she seemed to recognize the trio from somewhere a long time ago. No matter. The future of the Charrl was paramount: the Hive must survive at whatever cost.

She began to wade out to the TARDIS, rocking to and fro as the wind-swept waves tossed her back and forth.

'She'll drown if she goes any further!' screeched Charlie.

'No, she won't,' said Ace. 'All she wants to do is get to the TARDIS.'

'Benny,' called Popov. 'You must not do this!'

Benny hissed.

'Benny! Come back to us!' yelled Ace. 'Remember who you are! You're Bernice Summerfield! You're not a bloody insect! Bring the TVG back to us!'

Benny stopped at the door of the TARDIS and looked once more at the woman in the strange combat suit, her hair tossed in the wind and rain, who was running down the steps of the Embankment towards her.

She knew her.

'Ace?'

Ace reached the mudflat and, followed by Popov and Charlie, began to wade through the betossed waters of the Thames towards Benny.

'Professor Summerfield!' Khan's voice boomed out above the howl of the wind and the crashing of the thunder.

'Crikey, now we're done for!' said Charlie as all four of them looked up at the imposing figure of Khan, silhouetted in the lighting flare.

'The Charrl must survive!' he cried. 'The greatest race the Universe has ever spawned must not be allowed to die. Fulfil your destiny, Professor Summerfield! Restore the wand! Reunite the TARDIS with its true self!'

Benny seemed confused, torn between the power of the Charrl, and the urgent pleas of her friend, Ace, who was almost upon her. She slowly took the TARDIS key from the chain around her neck and opened the doors.

'Benny!' Ace pleaded. 'Don't do it!'

'Professor Summerfield, open the Great Divide!'

In a flash Benny made her decision. She dived into the TARDIS, and in one swift motion reconnected the Time Vector Generator to the two sockets which she had never noticed before, and which had been bored into the inside wall of the TARDIS like wormholes.

The night sky lit up with a tremendous flash of lighting, and the thunder deafened them all as the elements themselves were disturbed and disorientated by the unparalleled influx of energies.

Tachyons and luxons, hadrons and muons, quarks and antiquarks, photons and gravitrons, all collided and coalesced as they rushed from every corner of time and space, even from anti-time and anti-space, to give form, definition and purpose once more to the Doctor's TARDIS.

The powers released were too much for Benny to withstand and she was thrown out of the police box, to land in the churning waters of the Thames. Ace splashed over to her and lifted her head out of the water. The least she could do was save Benny from drowning, she thought. *Though from the looks of things we're all done for now!*

Above the sound of the lashing wind and rain the air was filled with another sound, the noise Ace always associated with dematerialization. But this time it was the re-birth cry of the TARDIS, as the old shattered police box was reunited with its true self, that inter- and infra-dimensional machine which had been suspended for too long outside of reality in the Vortex.

The sound of the TARDIS was drowned out by another harsher sound, and Ace looked up to the Embankment. Khan was standing there, arms outstretched to the wind and the rain, visibly drinking in the energies released as the TARDIS became once more a time machine.

He laughed maniacally, the laugh of a man who had finally gained what he most desired, the laugh not of a Faust, but of a Mephistopheles who had won the wager with his very own devil.

Antýkhon

The opaque globe exploded in a fury of sparks and shattered glass, and the nine Chronomancers who had sat around the globe for thousands of years sank into dust, their life-long sacrifice finally over. The Hive exploded with the chittering and chirruping and leg-clicking of thousands of Charrl as they all realized that the Great Divide was finally stabilized, and open to the Charrl was a new colony world.

Ch'tizz turned to Muldwych, and her normally rasping monotone voice was breathless with excitement. 'You have done it, Muldwych!' she cried. 'You kept your promise! You have granted the Charrl their survival.'

Muldwych's eyes were glazed with a joy all of his own. 'I suppose I have . . . ' he said.

He looked over at the old police box in the corner. It had remained resolutely unchanged but no matter: the path to Earth was now open not only to the Charrl but to himself as well.

'The TARDIS on Earth is whole once more,' he said. 'Free again to travel throughout all of space and time . . . '

'The TARDIS? The blue box?' *So that is what the Mammal was after!*

'The Great Divide is safe to cross over now,' said Muldwych, changing the subject.

'And when may we begin our next Great Migration?'

Muldwych's eyes twinkled. 'Well, there's no time like the present now, is there?'

Benny felt the rain beating down on her face and opened her eyes. Ace was holding her, looking at her in concern. She had dragged her to one of the mudflats on the banks of the Thames.

'Ace? What happened?'

'You've just let the bad guys win, that's all,' she said through gritted teeth.

'Miss Ace, look at Khan!' said Popov and pointed to the Embankment.

'What's happening?' asked Popov. Khan was *glowing* now as he sucked in the energies released from the TARDIS's rebirth. His laugh rose ever louder above the sound of the elements.

'I've got a very bad feeling about this . . . ' said Ace.

Benny looked curiously at her, and then back at Khan. She remembered something she had said to him a few days ago: *So what's in it for you, Khan? . . . Don't try and kid me you're doing all this for a bunch of overgrown insects . . . Your ambitions are a hell of a lot more basic than that . . .*

'He's not interested in the Charrl at all,' she suddenly realized. 'He's absorbing the time energies of the TARDIS . . . '

Suddenly Khan let out a blood-curdling scream of agony, and his whole body seemed to be ablaze with energy. The air was rapidly filled with the terrible stench of burning flesh.

'It's gone wrong,' Benny breathed. 'He can't stand the power.'

'Look at Khan!' said Charlie.

Khan was writhing in agony, his body transfixed in an unearthly light, so great that both banks of the Thames were illuminated in its horrible unnatural brilliance.

Finally with a scream that Ace, Benny and Charlie would remember for the rest of their lives, Jared Khan exploded, disappearing in a blazing conflagration of temporal and supra-spacial elements.

'He's done himself in!' gasped Charlie.

'Like an overloaded fuse,' said Benny. 'He couldn't stand the power . . . '

Through the driving rain, Ace looked at the TARDIS. The light on its stacked roof was flashing, signalling an imminent take-off. She looked back at the space where Jared Khan had stood.

'No, he hasn't!' she cried and stumbled to her feet, dragging Benny and Charlie with her. They raced over to the TARDIS, whose engines were already signalling its imminent departure.

Ace grabbed around Benny's neck for her keychain, but there was no need. The doors, which had closed after the TARDIS had been restored to its state as a time machine, blasted open of their own accord.

Without a word of explanation Ace shoved Benny and Charlie through the open doors, and dived in after them. The doors slammed shut.

As Popov, Seeba and Korin stared dumbfounded from the banks of the Thames, the TARDIS dematerialized.

Part Four

THE TARDIS

[illegible]

[illegible]

[illegible] this gun ready [illegible] Charlie [illegible]

[illegible]

[illegible] wasn't [illegible]

[illegible] only [illegible] the TARDIS would have [illegible]

Benny moved around the TARDIS. There was something wrong. The interior lighting was rising and falling in an uneasy, irregular rhythm; in the centre of the console the instrumentation contained within the [illegible] time rotor was flashing [illegible]

[illegible] within the [illegible] of the TARDIS the dreaded [illegible]

Benny [illegible] was [illegible] on [illegible] by [illegible] leading to the [illegible] of the time machine, [illegible]

'What's happening?'

'We're being haunted, that's what,' said Charlie.

Accompanied by the scanner [illegible] panels slowly opened. The screen was filled with the face of the man they had all thought had finally been destroyed.

'Khan!'

'[illegible]' Benny demanded. 'We saw you die!'

'The physical body of [illegible] Khan has died,' the man answered, and his voice – stronger, deeper and wider than

Chapter 23

'Yeah, we know, it's bigger inside than out,' said Ace non-chalantly as Charlie stared around the control chamber in awe. 'You should see the rest of it . . . '

'There's nowt left that's going to amaze me any more,' the young street urchin said philosophically. 'Bloody great walkin' talkin' insects what appear out of nowhere; magic wands; and ladies who give me mam more money than we had in our lives before – I've seen it all now!'

'That's the spirit!' Ace turned to Benny. 'We only just made it,' she said. 'Another few seconds and the TARDIS would have dematerialized and we'd've lost her forever.'

Benny looked around the TARDIS: there was something wrong. The interior lighting was rising and falling in an uneasy, irregular rhythm; in the centre of the console the instrumentation contained within the rising transparent time rotor was flashing ominously.

From deep within the centre of the TARDIS the dreaded tolling of a bell began.

Benny shivered; the temperature was descending rapidly: on the panels of the control console levers were moving by themselves; the door leading to the interior of the time machine, opened and closed, opened and closed.

'What's happening?'

'We're being haunted, that's what!' said Charlie.

Ace pointed to the scanner, whose twin panels slowly opened. The screen was filled with the face of the man they had all thought had finally been destroyed.

'Khan!'

'Where are you?' Benny demanded. 'We saw you die!'

'The physical body of Jared Khan has died,' the man answered, and his voice – stronger, deeper and wilder than anyone had heard it before – resounded throughout the time machine; even down to the Cloister Room itself, and the secret chambers at the very heart of the TARDIS where the Doctor had never allowed anyone to venture. Indeed, the voice of Jared Khan seemed to come from not one single source, but from the very fabric of the time machine itself.

'It was an old body, one that should have died seven hundred years ago,' continued Khan. 'Long before the Queen of the Charrl gave me unnatural life to help her in her quest for survival. Long before the Doctor cured me of the wasting sickness, and sent me on the unending journey down the bonny, bonny road.'

I might have known he'd be behind this somewhere, thought Benny.

'But now I have a new body, one that will last me forever,' continued Khan. 'One that possesses power without bourne and existence beyond all time and space . . . '

'What's he mean?' asked Charlie.

Benny and Ace looked at each other, as a terrifying suspicion dawned, and then down at the TARDIS controls which were moving by themselves.

'He's taking over the TARDIS!' Benny suddenly realized. 'That's what he wanted all along! Not to help the Charrl! Not even to gain eternal life! *He wants to become the TARDIS!'*

'Then you got to stop him,' said Charlie simply, not sure what Benny was talking about, only somehow recognizing the danger that a Jared Khan, possessed of the almost-infinite powers of a TARDIS, would pose to creation.

One of the control panels erupted in a shower of sparks: on the screen Khan frowned.

'What's happening?' asked Benny.

'The TARDIS isn't going to let go without a struggle,' said Ace. Benny looked at her bemused.

'I've been in the TARDIS longer than you,' Ace stated simply. 'I know the TARDIS better. She's like a living creature –'

'– And Khan is like a virus in her bloodstream,' said Benny. 'A virus she's trying to eject.'

The floor beneath them heaved, as the TARDIS fought with

Khan for possession of her power. Banks of instruments which lined the walls of the control chamber exploded or shattered; the roundelled walls themselves bent and buckled under the enormous strain.

Along the seemingly infinite corridors of the time machine ran rivers of flame; in other areas the temperature dropped so rapidly that the walls became encrusted with a thick layer of frost. Rooms were ejected mercilessly, one by one, as the TARDIS tried unsuccessfully to dispel Khan from her system.

'We must do something!' cried Benny and looked, for once, to the younger woman for guidance. 'We must help the TARDIS!'

Ace reached for the control panel, which exploded at her touch in a burst of unchecked artron energy.

'We've got to fight Khan on his own ground,' she said. 'We've got to enter the mind of the TARDIS and fight him there!'

'But how?' asked Benny, but Ace was already racing to one of the roundelled panels in the TARDIS wall. She opened it and pulled out a silver headset.

'Remember I've been with the Professor longer than you,' she said. 'He's used this before – to tap into the TARDIS' telepathic circuits . . .'

Benny took the headset from Ace, and raised it to her head. Ace protested.

'I got us into this mess, Ace,' Benny declared. 'I think I'd better try and get us out of it, don't you?'

'You're crazy,' said Ace. 'I know the TARDIS better than you –'

'But I know Khan better,' Benny insisted. 'I made contact with his mind, remember, when I was a prisoner. If anyone's going to do battle with Khan, it had better be me.'

Ignoring Ace's protests, Benny slipped on the headset.

Chapter 24

The fog lifted from Benny's eyes and she looked around her. She was still in the console room, but of Ace and Charlie there was no sign. The control chamber was cold, and eerily silent; not a tick, not a whir, not even the ubiquitous hum of the tens of thousands of instruments required to regulate the time machine's journey through time and space.

The time rotor in the centre of the console was still, and the LED displays on the control panels dark. She looked over at the Doctor's eagle-shaped lectern and frowned: she could have sworn she saw it winking at her.

She turned and walked towards the door which led to the interior of the ship. Her footsteps echoed on the control floor.

'I wouldn't go down in there, if I were you,' advised the eagle.

'Sorry, I have to,' Benny replied. 'I've got to stop Khan.'

'At least he has a love of beauty,' the eagle said grumpily. 'The Doctor never appreciated me. Took me all around the Universe with him, he did, and then dumped me in an old storeroom without so much as a by-your-leave when he turned into that white-haired chap in the fancy clothes. Take care it doesn't happen to you!'

'Look, I don't have time to talk to a piece of antique furniture,' Benny pointed out, but the eagle fell silent and unseeing again. Benny opened the door.

And walked right into a scholar's study. Hundreds of books were piled on the floor, reaching nearly up to the ceiling, and on a long wooden table, several vile-smelling potions were brewing. Above the table there was a window, through which she could see in the distance the great dome of the cathedral of Notre Dame.

Benny looked behind her. The TARDIS had vanished, and she found herself staring at a rough wooden door. A calendar on the wall stated that the date was 3 November 1867. A slight cough made her turn around.

A small wizened old man was sitting hunched over his desk, reading a large ancient volume. He heard the rustle of Benny's skirts, registered her presence and looked up.

'Hello,' he said, and grinned, showing a mouth of decayed and blackened teeth. His breath reeked.

'Who are you?' asked Benny 'Where am I?'

'My name is Eliphas Levi,' the old man wheezed. 'And I'm about to "die". And you're in the TARDIS.'

Benny pointed through the window at Notre Dame.

'Oh you noticed that, did you?' said Levi. 'Well, we're in Paris as well. When you're in the TARDIS you can be everywhere and nowhere at the same time. It's what you make of it.' He tapped his head. 'All in the mind, you see. That's why all physical conflict here is impossible. You need your wits about you . . . '

'You said you were going to die . . . '

'That's right. I've died many times in the past few centuries,' Levi said. 'I've an appointment, you see, in London.'

Slowly Levi's back straightened and he became more imposing. His figure filled out, and his rheumy eyes became bright and piercing.

'Khan!'

'I'm afraid I can't allow you to take the TARDIS away from me, Professor Summerfield,' he stated plainly. 'I need it far more than you ever will . . . '

'Damn you, Khan!' cried Benny and grabbed him by the lapels of his coat. 'Don't you care about anyone else but yourself?'

'No,' he replied. 'I must survive. Nothing else matters.'

Benny shook Khan, and before her eyes he vanished, leaving her holding an empty sack of clothes. Shaking her head in disbelief Benny walked over and opened the wooden door of the study.

And found herself in a large assembly hall, of the type which was once to be found in every major public school in England. It was Prize-Giving Day, and the assembly hall was packed with children dressed in Victorian school uniform, and their proud parents.

Benny was dressed in her 25th-century clothes of an orange tunic and navy-blue leggings; but it was the fact that her parents weren't with her that made her feel most out of place.

Up on the stage Ace, dressed in a prim Victorian dress and wearing an academic gown and mortar board, was reading out the names of girls and calling them up one by one to receive their prizes from a kindly old lady in a wheelchair.

'And the prize for outstanding achievement in history and archaeology goes to – Professor Bernice Summerfield.'

'Go on, Benny,' the young girl sitting next to her said. 'Go up and get your prize!'

Dazed, Benny stood up and made her way through the crowd of cheering schoolchildren and parents to the stage where Ace greeted her warmly, and pecked her on the cheek. She unfurled a roll of parchment and addressed the rest of the school.

'Honours in ancient Terran history, and Martian archaeology,' she read out, and behind her Benny winced in embarrassment. 'A professorial thesis on Draconian culture . . . '

She turned round to look at Benny, and continued to read: 'And a degree in forging a false set of documents.' She turned back to the audience. ' "Professor" Summerfield is a con merchant, kids.'

The chant of 'cheat, cheat, cheat' came from the audience.

'That's right, girls, Summerfield is a cheat. And we all know what we do with cheats here, don't we?'

Cheat, cheat, cheat.

Benny had been found out. She felt Ace's iron grip lead her to the lady in the wheelchair.

'Come and receive your prize, Summerfield.'

The lady in the wheelchair had vanished and in her place there stood a burly, masked executioner. Her surroundings, too, had suddenly changed and now she found herself on a raised wooden platform, her hands tied behind her back. She was kneeling in front of a guillotine.

Below her a mass of angry French citizens jeered at her and demanded her death. Benny looked spitefully at them, and in the crowd noticed a bewigged man, dressed in the aristocratic finery which in Revolutionary Paris should have earned him a death sentence also.

The executioner offered her a blindfold, which she refused with contempt, and she felt herself being pushed forward and her head being laid on the block.

An expectant hush fell on the crowd as Ace read out the charges:

'For deceit and calumny, for equivocation and mendacity beyond belief, and also for telling a whole load of porkies, we sentence "Professor" Bernice Summerfield to death!'

The silver guillotine blade whooshed down, cleanly separating Benny's head from her body.

Chapter 25

Miles away from Paris, France, the aristocratic observer from the crowd sat on a rock, overlooking an empty grave, and held Benny's decapitated head before him. 'Alas, poor Benny, I knew her well . . . '

'I'll take that, thank you very much,' said a headless corpse, now dressed in regulation 25th-century combat gear, and snatched the head from him, placing it firmly on her own shoulders.

The aristocrat betrayed no surprise at seeing a walking decapitated corpse, let alone one which could somehow speak.

'So you survived?' he yawned.

'You'll have to do better than that, Khan,' said Benny, and the aristocrat frowned. 'Just who are you this time?'

The aristocrat stood up and affected a courtly bow. 'Count Alessandro di Cagliostro, at your service, ma'am.'

'Who?' Benny was unimpressed.

'I was an Italian, born in 1743; they say I died in 1795,' he explained. 'But then I had an appointment somewhere else . . . I spent most of my days selling bottles of a fake Elixir of Life, and searching for the true one.' He gestured around the rocky wasteland expansively. 'And now I have found it.'

'The TARDIS?'

'By becoming one with the TARDIS I shall be granted life eternal, and final surcease from the agonies that have pursued me down the ages . . . '

'Down the ages?' asked Benny. 'Look, just how long have you lived, Khan?'

'I was born over seven hundred years ago . . . ' Khan/Cagliostro explained.

'Then you already have eternal life.'

'Eternal life? To be trapped in a shattered shell of a body such as mine? To endure this endless wasting? When I can gain power without measure, and knowledge without limits.

'I must have the TARDIS, Professor Summerfield – and I shall not allow you – or anyone else – to hinder me!'

'I will find some way to stop you if it's the last thing I do. I owe it to the Doctor. I won't let you take away his TARDIS.'

'The Doctor! *His* TARDIS?' sneered Khan/Cagliostro. 'Who owns who, I wonder. I've known of the Doctor and his TARDIS for a long time. How much do you know about either of them, Professor Summerfield? Beware them – they are as devious and manipulative as each other!'

Khan/Cagliostro laughed at the uncomprehending Benny and then jumped into the hollow grave. When Benny peered over the gravemouth he had vanished.

'Damn!' She surveyed the rocky wasteland before her. A little way off there was a pebbled road which forked in three different directions. One road was rocky; one meandered through a field of white flowers; and the third stretched out wide and fine and headed towards faraway hills.

And where's the Yellow Brick Road? Benny asked herself, and looked up: if she had suddenly seen a tiny cottage falling out of the rust-coloured sky she wouldn't have been at all surprised.

As she pondered which turning to take, she heard a strange bell-like voice starting to sing. She turned around, but there was no one there. Still the voice continued to sing. It was a voice, a female voice – and a song – that she'd never heard before.

> O see ye not yon narrow road,
>   So thick beset wi' thorns and briars?
> That is the Path of Righteousness,
>   Though after it but few inquires.

'Who's there?' asked Benny. No reply. The unseen voice continued:

> And see ye not yon braid, braid road,
>   That lies across the lily leven?
> That is the Path to Wickedness,
>   Though some call it the Road to Heaven.

And see ye not yon bonny road
  That winds about the fernie brae?
That is the road to fair Elfland,
  Where thou and I this night maun gae.

Not sure whether the voice she could hear was a trap of Khan's, not even certain whether the voice was real or imaginary, Benny set her foot upon the narrow road.

In a flash of energy her surroundings changed again. The rocky wasteland had gone, as had the two other roads. She was now standing on a narrow rock bridge which spanned an abyss between two cliffs. Far below her a blood-red sea churned and toiled.

Waiting for her on the opposite side was a huge spider, at least three times as big as Benny. And four times as nasty.

'You can only go forwards,' the Spider called over, in a warm and reassuringly feminine voice which was totally belied by her hideous appearance. 'Take a look behind you.'

Benny turned and saw that the cliff on her side had vanished, leaving behind nothing but a raw and aching white void. Even as the Spider was speaking the void seemed to be growing, slowly eating away at the bridge centimetre by centimetre, approaching Benny, leaving her no choice but to go forwards.

'Come across,' the Spider said. 'I won't hurt you.'

Oh yes?

The Spider sniffed. 'That's the trouble with humans. Always judging by outward appearances. It's what underneath that counts. I can't imagine why they're one of my favourite species . . . '

Benny cast a nervous look behind her: the bridge was slowly being eaten away.

'You've got two choices,' the Spider said gently. 'You can trust me and come across. Or you can jump down into the waters of Usher's Well where you will die . . . '

You're a figment of the imagination, Benny thought. *You don't really exist. I can wish you out of existence.*

'I'm afraid you can't,' said the Spider, reading her thoughts. 'Mister Khan is in control here now.' She sniffed haughtily. 'Nasty little man that he is. The only ally you have now is the

TARDIS herself. And she's fighting back . . . You have to decide for yourself whether I'm on Mister Khan's side, or on the TARDIS's.'

Accepting the inevitable, Benny started to walk across the bridge. The Spider urged her on, cooing at her gently as a mother would to her young.

When Benny had almost reached the other side, she noticed that the Spider was gnawing on something.

'Oh this?' said the Spider, and plucked a greasy bone out of her giant mandibles with a claw. 'Just a snack. I'm always hungry, you see; day in, day out I can just never seem to get enough to eat.'

She waved the bone in Benny's face, who turned away in revulsion; burnt and blackened meat was still hanging off the bone.

'This one belonged to someone called Adric,' she said. 'A bit overdone for my taste, but sometimes you can't afford to be too choosy.'

She indicated a pile of bones a little way off.

'And those used to be called Katarina – or was it Margaret? I never can remember those stupid girls' names.' She pointed to another pile of bones. 'And those belonged to a lad called Raphael – I'm worried about those, though: they glow so.

'But the greatest feast of them all will be the Seven Planets. Imagine the meat on those! Would you care to join me in the banquet?'

Benny shuddered, and grew pale at the thought of the Spider gnawing on the bones of all those whose trust in the Doctor had lost them their lives.

The Spider seemed disappointed. 'But you must join me in my meal,' she insisted, and her tone changed. 'After all, you're a trusting soul. You could make a very tasty dessert.'

A claw lashed out at Benny, almost causing her to lose her balance. She took a step back onto the non-existent bridge, and with a yelp fell headlong into the fierce waters below.

The Spider peered over the edge of the cliff at Benny's rapidly descending body. 'How unfortunate she couldn't stay for tea,' she said, and resumed her chewing of Adric's bones.

Benny fell with a sickening *crash!* into the blood-red waters of Usher's Well. As she came up for the first time she discovered with revulsion that she was actually swimming in real blood.

Inhuman hands reached out of the water, and pulled her under for a second time. In the blood's opacity she could not see who her attackers were, only feel their hands clawing and ripping at her. Furiously she tried to fight them off as they began to drag her down for a third and final time, and Benny began to lose consciousness.

Skreeeeeeeeeeeeeeeek!

Benny turned her head in the direction of the cry. Something was swimming through the water towards Benny, sending up a spray of blood in its wake. She watched through almost dreaming eyes as the creature dived beneath the surface and attacked her would-be murderers with its pincers, and stinging tentacles.

The water churned as the creature snipped and snatched at her attackers, killing them as effectively and as mercilessly as a – well, as a Dalek . . .

Then Benny was aware of a tentacle being placed gently, almost lovingly, about her neck as the creature pulled her ashore.

As she sat up on the dry land, she noticed that she was once again wearing her nightgown and Margaret's coat and that neither garment was either wet, or blood-stained.

She turned to look at and thank her rescuer, and gasped in astonishment and horror as she saw the creature which had saved her. It squawked a farewell at her and then dived back into the sea.

'Things flow so about here!' remarked a passing Wolf who was rowing a tiny coracle *through* the heather-covered ground, seemingly with a total disregard for any of the normal laws of physics.

The Wolf 'moored' his boat close to Benny.

'Hello, Mister Wolf,' Benny said warily; after all, even she had heard the story of Red Riding Hood.

'You don't trust me, do you?' growled the Wolf.

'Not half!'

The Wolf tut-tutted. 'I suppose I'll have to change again then,' he complained, and before Benny's eyes he transformed himself into a Lamb. 'There. Is that better?' he bleated. Benny agreed that it was.

'A Lamb in Wolf's clothing, that's what I am!' giggled the Lamb in a distinctly feminine voice. 'Two for the price of one, Benny, two for the price of one! Never judge by appearances, Professor Summerfield!'

Benny nodded over at the 'waters' of Usher's Well. 'That creature who just saved my life . . . Was it what I thought it was?'

'That's right,' said the Lamb. 'A Kaled mutant.'

'I've just been saved by a baby Dalek?' Even in the topsy-turvy world that was the TARDIS that was hard to believe.

'A long time ago the Doctor had the opportunity to destroy the entire Dalek race,' explained the Lamb. 'But he didn't. If you like, you can think of that mutant as an expression of the Doctor's compassion for all Creation.'

'And what about that Spider?'

'Ah,' said the Lamb sadly. 'That was an expression of something much darker . . .'

'So what are you an "expression" of then?' Benny demanded. 'In Earth mythology the Lamb was always a symbol of Christ.'

The Lamb chuckled. 'Nothing so holy as that, I'm afraid. I'm just a Lamb, that's all.' The Lamb climbed back into her coracle, and started rowing through the ground again. 'Take care, Benny, take care . . .'

Benny waved goodbye, and a prim, upper-class voice behind her said: 'She shouldn't really do that, you know.'

'Do what?' asked Benny.

' . . . If a person is going to sail at all then she should at least have the good manners to do it on the water. Breaking the laws of physics like that might give a young child any amount of bad ideas. I mean, just look at Gallifrey . . .'

Benny turned around and saw a stern English Nanny pushing an old-fashioned pram on the banks of what, if the late 21st-century developers hadn't filled it in, Benny would have recognized as the Serpentine in London's Hyde Park. From within the pram Benny could hear the gurgling of a Baby.

Suddenly Benny forgot her mission in the TARDIS, forgot the threat of Khan and the Charrl, forgot even the Doctor and

Ace. All her adventures and experiences meant nothing to her; all she wanted was to hold and cuddle the Baby.

She looked hopefully at the Nanny.

'May I?'

The Nanny sniffed. 'Don't see why not! After all, it's the child you might have one day!'

Benny peered into the pram to see the beaming face of a small baby boy. She winked at it, and chattered to it in baby-talk.

'Can I pick him up, please?' she asked.

'As you please, Miss Summerfield, as you please.'

Gently, as if she was picking up a piece of fragile china, or unearthing a particularly ancient artefact, she lifted the Baby up in her arms.

She began to croon softly to it, and the Baby giggled happily.

'He's lovely,' she said to the Nanny. 'Whose is he?'

The Nanny harrumphed contemptuously, as if she couldn't care less, and turned away. Benny shrugged, and held the Baby more tightly to her.

He's the loveliest, most gentle, most fulfilling thing I've ever seen, she thought dreamily. *To be a parent, to be responsible for creating another human being. To know that the child depends on you, and you alone, to teach it, and guide it through its first stumbling years, and to be the centre around which that child's life revolves. To know that without you that child would be nothing . . .*

She felt a terrible pain in her neck. The Baby she had been holding had suddenly changed into a ferocious Charrl, ripping at her neck and eagerly scooping out her flesh with its razor-sharp mandibles.

'Help me!' she cried, as her punctured jugular vein pumped out blood, but the Nanny simply turned away from her.

'It's nothing to do with me now. You picked it up; you made yourself responsible for it. It's your Baby now,' she said. 'You're responsible for it now.'

Benny reached out in an attempt to overpower the Charrl and throw it off her. With a mighty heave, she lifted the thrashing insect off her neck and was about to fling it to the ground –

– when she saw that it had changed once more into a gentle, gurgling baby boy.

She shuddered; another second and she would have thrown the innocent child into the freezing water of the Serpentine.

'Oh my God, I'm sorry,' she said. She lifted one hand to her neck: there was no trace of a wound. She clutched the Baby once more to her breast.

And it transformed itself this time into a Kaled mutant, quite possibly the very same mutant that had saved her life earlier, but this time choking the life out of her.

She wrenched if off her body in horror and disgust –

– and it changed once more into a gurgling, defenceless Baby.

'You've accepted the Child,' said the Nanny.

'So?'

'Now you must live with it,' the Nanny continued.

Only it wasn't the Nanny who was speaking. It was the Lamb. And Benny suddenly remembered someone else who had accepted another sort of Child an unimaginably long time ago. And the Doctor was still living with the consequences of that decision.

She hugged the Baby to her breast –

– where it changed instantly into a Hyena, ripping at her flesh, tearing at her breasts, until the blood poured down her nightdress.

And Benny panicked, and instinctively tore the Hyena off her.

And it became a Baby again.

'Well, Benny?' asked the Lamb. 'Which are you going to choose? The Innocent? Or the Guilty?'

Benny clutched the Baby to her, and it changed into a writhing, hissing Serpent. Its fangs tore mercilessly into her tender white flesh.

'Benny?'

The Lamb was worried.

Benny smiled. She felt the poison of the Snake's venom seep into her bloodstream. Its action was fast, and reached Benny's heart within seconds.

Her heart convulsed. A few seconds later the Snake venom reached her brain and caused a massive seizure and Benny gasped her very last breath.

Bernice Summerfield, archaeologist, time-traveller and sometime lady, died.

Chapter 26

The Lamb looked down on Benny's corpse with concern. The Snake was still there, writhing about on her body, sucking greedily at her blood, and at the same time injecting more venom into Benny's complaisant body.

This wasn't supposed to happen! the Lamb reminded herself. 'Benny?' she bleated, 'Benny, speak to me!'

Benny sat up. ' "Peace, peace!" ' she misquoted. ' "Dost thou not see my baby at my breast, That sucks the nurse awake?" '

'Shakespeare?' asked the Lamb.

'No, Summerfield,' said Benny, and tossed the Snake off her body. 'Khan's playing at my emotions, but he hasn't won yet.' She frowned. 'What's that noise?'

'I don't hear anything,' said the Lamb.

'Listen,' said Benny and turned to the Lamb.

Who was no longer standing there, she noticed.

In fact, neither was the Serpentine, nor Hyde Park for that matter.

Across the misty moor a Scottish piper was approaching her, and the sound she could hear was the ungodly howl of his bagpipes.

'Will you stop that racket!' Benny cried out. 'I can't hear myself think!'

The piper stopped his playing. 'It's the Highlander's Lament,' he explained. 'I'm playing it for all those who lost their lives here . . . '

Benny looked around at the deserted and bleak moor where she now found herself. 'Here? Where's here?'

'Culloden,' continued the piper. 'Thousands died here when Bonnie Prince Charlie was finally defeated by the Duke of Cumberland.'

Culloden, remembered Benny. *The Doctor was here once. He had a companion who he'd met at Culloden.*

'That's right,' said the piper, reading her thoughts. 'But they've gone now. I just missed them again. But there will be other times, in other places . . . . '

'You're Khan,' Benny realized.

'I'm just a poor Scots piper, come to watch the puppet show,' he said, and indicated a ramshackle wooden stall, incongruously placed in the middle of the moor. Benny strode over and the piper vanished into the mists.

As she approached the stall so it grew bigger – or she grew smaller, she wasn't quite sure – and by the time she had reached it she was the same size as the puppets.

It was a sort of Punch and Judy show, performed by marionettes, and she watched, captivated, as Punch beat up Judy, and the Policeman tried unsuccessfully to stop them.

So entranced and entertained was she, that it was minutes – or was it hours? In the TARDIS you never could be sure – before she realized that the puppets were, in fact, real human beings.

And that the puppet bashing the hell out of a surprised Judy with a baseball bat was, in fact, Ace.

And that the other puppets were all faces she recognized from one of her periodic forays into the TARDIS's data core: Vicki, Nyssa, Peri, Steven, all former companions of the Doctor, and each one left by him to an uncertain fate.

She looked up into the sky, at the puppet-master pulling the strings. Sure enough, it was a puppet itself, a grotesquely grinning representation of the Doctor.

'The show must go on!' cackled the Doctor-Puppet.

'Not if I can help it!' she cried out, and seized an enormous pair of scissors she found lying on the ground.

She ran over to the puppets and cut their strings one by one, freeing them from the Doctor's control.

'Now you've gone and spoilt my little game,' sulked the Doctor-Puppet and faded out of existence.

Benny went over to the fallen puppets. Ace, Vicki, Steven, Nyssa and Peri had all fallen to the ground the instant Benny had cut their strings; they were dead. Before her eyes they turned into grinning rag dolls.

'That's what comes from cutting people's strings,' said the Lamb sadly.

'Is he really a Puppet-Master?' asked Benny, unperturbed by the Lamb's sudden reappearance.

'It's up to you to decide,' said the Lamb. 'He could be. Then again Khan could be trying to make you question your faith in the Doctor. Which do you think it is?'

'I trust the Doctor,' said Benny, after some serious thought. *I think.*

'Good,' bleated the Lamb and looked up at the sky. 'It's getting dark now. I must be going . . . ' she said and leapt away off into the shadows.

Within a matter of seconds the sun had set and it was night and Benny found herself on a dark expansive plain. In the distance she saw a light coming from a hut perched on top of a high hill. She was about to make her way to it, when a Lion crossed her path.

'Good evening to you,' he said in a high-pitched, slightly effeminate voice.

'Evening,' said Benny and looked at the Lion warily.

'Oh you needn't be frightened of me,' the Lion said. 'I'm dead.'

'Silly of me,' Benny riposted. 'I should have known.'

'The last Lion on Earth, that's me,' he said proudly. 'We're now officially extinct. Got shot on this very plain.'

'And where's that?'

'Place used to be known as Ngorongoro, in a country they once called Tanzania,' he said, and cocked his head to the hill. 'And that place up there they still call Mount Kukūruk. Chap called Muldwych lives there.'

'Don't you mind being dead?' asked Benny.

'Not really. After all I still survive in the TARDIS,' he said. 'And I deserved to die . . . '

'What do you mean?'

'I was very hungry, you see. Attacked a human; shouldn't have done, of course, there were still some zebra around at that time. He shot me; it was his right. Kill or be killed, it's the law of the jungle, the law of survival.'

'There are other ways.'

'Sometimes it's necessary for one thing to die so that another thing can live,' said the Lion. 'Remember that, Benny.'

Before her eyes the flesh dropped off the Lion until all that was left of it was a pile of old decaying bones. Benny shuddered: she knew that everything she was experiencing was nothing but a fantasy, conjured up by either Khan or the TARDIS herself, but that still didn't make it any easier. With a weary heart she began the long trudge up to Muldwych's hut on the top of Mount Kukūruk.

It seemed to take her about half an hour to reach the hut. When she did, she creaked open the door – and immediately gagged as the stench of dead and rotting meat reached her nose.

She was in a slaughter-house. Blood swilled the floor, and hung up on hooks along the wall were slabs of dead meat: not just of animals either: the dead eyes of several young women stared down lifelessly at her, each one of them unfortunate victims of the Charrl.

'You're just in time,' came a gruff masculine voice, and Benny turned in the direction of the voice to see a burly Butcher, his white apron stained reddish-brown with blood. He was holding an enormous meat cleaver in his hand.

On the Butcher's slab in front of him lay the Lamb. Benny shuddered, and made a move to stop the Butcher from bringing his cleaver down onto the Lamb's neck.

'You don't understand, Benny,' bleated the Lamb. 'Sometimes it's necessary for one thing to die . . . '

'So that another thing can live,' Benny finished. 'I know . . . '

'He can slaughter the Lamb,' the Lamb said meaningfully, 'but can he kill the Wolf?'

'I don't understand,' said Benny, but the Lamb had no time to reply as the Butcher brought the meat cleaver down onto her neck. Hot blood spurted out of the carcass, covering Benny.

'You bastard!' she cried. 'She was my friend!'

The Butcher sneered. 'Your friend? What did you ever do for her?'

'Well, I . . . I . . . '

'Precisely! You're just like all the others,' the Butcher

continued. 'Always taking and never giving. Even with the Doctor – what have you ever done for him?'

Benny turned away in disgust and left the hut. Instead of Mount Kukūruk she found herself walking into a ramshackle old empty cinema. Ace was waiting for her, dressed in an usherette's uniform.

'Come on now,' she said. 'The main feature's about to start!' She escorted Benny to a threadbare seat in the centre of the auditorium.

Ace looked up at the projectionist's booth at the back of the theatre.

'OK, roll 'em!' she commanded and then looked back at Benny. 'Remember it's only a movie, it's not real,' she said and then reconsidered. 'Of course what you're experiencing now isn't real either. So maybe that does make the movie real after all . . . '

The lights went down and the flickering black-and-white image of a Scottish moor came up on the enormous screen. The movie was poorly lit and directed, Benny decided; but she also realized that she was watching a real event.

It was a tear-jerker, the tale of a young Scottish lad with only a few years to live, after having contracted a mysterious wasting illness. Of a young Scottish lad who came to a deal with a mysterious white lady.

The white lady promised the lad eternal life, a cure for his illness, and power unimaginable if he would perform one simple task: to track down a magic wand for her, a magic wand which would guarantee the survival of all her people.

Benny watched as the young man grew, pursuing the Doctor and his TARDIS down through the ages. She saw him as a precocious astrologer at the court of Kubilai Khan in China; a mystic at the court of Queen Elizabeth the First; a Scottish piper, an Italian count, a Jewish alchemist in Paris. A quest which had lasted seven hundred years with him always just one step behind the Doctor, always just one step behind the TARDIS which he needed to ensure his continued survival.

Finally she saw the young lad as Jared Khan, grinning maniacally at her from the cinema screen.

'I won't let you take the TARDIS from me, Professor

Summerfield,' he announced, 'I must survive!'

Khan's image reached out of the cinema screen and scooped Benny up in his enormous hand. He started to crush her body as Benny squirmed and tried to wriggle out of his grip.

'I will survive, Professor Summerfield!' he declared, and squeezed even more tightly. Benny felt her ribs caving in, piercing her lungs. Blood started to spurt out of her mouth.

'Ace!' she screamed, although the Usherette-Ace had long since vanished. 'Take me back! Take me back!'

Chapter 27

Benny came to in the devastated TARDIS control room. Ace and Charlie were bending over her in concern. Ace took the headset off her and helped her roughly to her feet.

'It's no good,' Benny said. 'Khan's gaining power by the minute. He'll soon be invincible.'

'Did you learn anything?' Ace asked. 'Anything that might help us stop him?'

'Only that it's sometimes necessary to kill one thing for another thing to survive . . . ' Benny said slowly.

Ace and Charlie stared at each other. 'Don't bother asking me, Charlie,' Ace shrugged. 'I don't know what she's talking about either . . . '

'I've got an idea . . . ' Benny said.

'That's wonderful,' Charlie cheered.

'Trouble is, I don't think you're going to like it . . . '

'Well, spit it out then!'

'When the TARDIS materialized in London, it transformed itself into a police box, so that Khan couldn't get at its temporal energies. Right?'

Ace nodded, when a frightening thought struck her. 'We can't disconnect the TVG again, Benny, not while we're in flight!'

'That's not what I'm suggesting, Ace,' she continued. 'I doubt we could even do it if we wanted to. Besides there would be nothing to stop someone reconnecting the TVG at a later date.'

'So what's your big idea?'

'Deprive Khan of his power source completely. Forever,' stated Benny coldly. 'We know that the TARDIS can reconfigure its internal dimensions infinitely . . . '

'Wait a minute, I don't like the sound of this . . . '

'We persuade the TARDIS to self-destruct!'

'My God, Charlie, the crazy cow wants to blow us all up,'

breathed Ace. 'There's got to be another way, Benny!'

'Any alternative suggestions will be gratefully accepted in the following few minutes we have left to us.'

Ace paced around the console room. 'You can't destroy the TARDIS. It's been my home for years.'

'You can't afford to be sentimental, Ace,' Benny pointed out rather pompously.

'Can't I just? The TARDIS isn't just a machine. It's a living person; it'd be like committing murder.'

Ace examined the instrument panels of the control console, as if they might provide her with an answer. 'Think! What would the Professor do?'

'Knowing the Doctor he's probably already done it and is just waiting for us to catch up with him!' said Benny, unwittingly echoing Ace's previous words.

'Yeah . . . ' said Ace. 'Wait a minute, that's it! Only it's not the Professor who's done it – it's the TARDIS!' Excitedly she started operating the controls.

'What are you doing?' asked Benny.

'Setting the co-ordinates.'

'You can do that?' Benny was impressed by the younger woman's knowledge.

'Course I can – I've watched the Professor enough times,' she said superiorly. 'Besides I've got some extra help!'

'Who?' asked Charlie.

'The TARDIS herself!'

'And just where do you think you're taking us?' asked Benny sternly.

'Antýkhon of course . . . When the TARDIS "crashed" it split itself into two, right? Well, there must have been a reason for it . . . '

'I thought it was to separate us, to keep you from getting the TVG.'

'Why? I might know more about the TARDIS than you do, but I still wouldn't have known what to do with the TVG. Khan's taking over the TARDIS – but he's only taking over half a TARDIS! The other half is waiting for us on Antýkhon! The TARDIS had planned it all along!'

' "Two for the price of one",' muttered Benny.

'What?'

'Oh, just something a Lamb said to me once . . . '

Ace drew Benny and Charlie's attention to the large central time rotor: it was slowly descending to a halt. They had arrived back on Antýkhon; Ace activated the scanner controls, and the panels on the screen slid open to show them the image of what was outside.

They had landed in the Hive – a Hive which was now strangely empty. Opposite them stood that part of the TARDIS which had bought Ace to Antýkhon.

'Now what?' asked Benny.

'I think it's being taken out of our hands now . . . ' said Ace.

The time machine shuddered as Khan became aware of the presence of another TARDIS. He reached out his mind, trying to embrace its power as he had done that of the original TARDIS, and in doing so relaxed his hold.

Inside the console room, the lights dimmed and the central time rotor blazed a fiery red. The air was filled with a curious wheezing noise, not the usual sound of dematerialization, but a deeper, more strained sound, like someone groaning in pain.

Ace, Benny and Charlie looked at the walls of the console room: they were bending and shimmering as the TARDIS tried to take advantage of Khan's momentary relaxation of power and expel the foreign intelligence which had dared to invade her very being.

Part of the console exploded in a flash of flame. On the scanner screen they watched the other TARDIS tremble – and then dematerialize.

'He's transferred himself to the other TARDIS!' said Benny. 'He's going to win after all!'

Charlie pointed to the LED display on the TARDIS's navigation board. 'What are them numbers changing for?' he asked.

Ace and Benny looked at each other. The TARDIS's co-ordinates were changing, seemingly by themselves. Ace shrugged at Benny.

'What do I do now?'

'This,' she said, and rammed down the main dematerialization lever.

As the TARDIS vanished from the surface of Antýkhon, Benny pointed to a small screen on the navigational panel which was flashing an urgent message. She didn't like the sound of it.

'Ace, what's a Time Ram?'

Ace's face turned even whiter than it was normally. She remembered something the Professor had once said, about one of the most dangerous manoeuvres a TARDIS could ever perform.

'It's when two objects occupy exactly the same place in both space and time . . . '

'That's impossible.'

'Exactly. This Universe ain't going to be big enough for the both of us . . . '

Somewhere in the Time Vortex, that indefinable somewhen which exists between all the known and unknown dimensions, a flash of energy appeared, shining in the unfathomable darkness like a tiny star.

In the eternal infinity of the Vortex, however, it was insignificant, the slightest ripple in the ever-changing, ever-unpredictable possibilities of time and space.

An infinitesimal fraction of a nanosecond later, another flash of energy tried to appear, attempted to occupy the same space as the first energy source.

For another fraction of a nanosecond the two shone brightly as one, each one jostling for position.

And then the second pinprick of energy was expelled, sent hurtling out of the Vortex, into the real world of space and time, and to its pre-ordained destruction.

Somewhere over the barren wastes of Tungasaku, in a land called Siberia on the last day of June 1908, the part of the TARDIS that she herself had willingly sacrificed to Jared Khan exploded.

And across the ages a Great Divide was opened . . .

* * *

Report from Nature *magazine, 29 May 1965*

The most spectacular meteor fall to be recorded in modern times occurred on June 30 1908 in the basin of the Podkanemaia River, Siberia, some miles to the north of Lake Baykal. It was seen in the cloudless sky over an area of about 1,500 km . . . The fall was accompanied by violent radiation and shock phenomena, the meteorological and geomagnetic fields were registered at points around the world . . .

No trace of a crater was found.

Chapter 28

The East End, London,
7.30 a.m., Saturday 24 April AD 1909

With the Great Divide now completely stabilized the Charrl were appearing in the East End in scores. Bellingham had been there to greet them and had provided a warehouse in which they could hide until enough of their number had crossed over.

Ch'tizz had been the first to arrive and she was supervising the operation with a deep sense of achievement. She had not failed her people or the Goddess: she had sworn to find them a new home and she had kept her word.

She turned to Muldwych. 'You have done us a great service, Muldwych. What can the Charrl do to repay you?'

'There's no reward I need from the Charrl, Your Majesty,' he said.

'But you helped us harness the energy of the Great Divide, trained our Chronomancers to reach back through time and contact the Khan Mammal . . . '

She looked suspiciously at the fat little man. 'Why have you helped us so, Muldwych?'

'I too need my freedom,' he replied. 'The survival of your race and my own are closely interlinked. For almost a thousand years I was stranded on Mount Kukūruk, an exile. Now with the Great Divide stabilized, and the TARDIS restored to its proper condition, I will at long last be allowed the freedom to travel in all space and time.'

As if on cue, the TARDIS materialized, and Ace, Benny and Charlie stepped out. Charlie clutched at Benny as he saw the figure of Ch'tizz.

Ace took in the situation instantly: Muldwych, Ch'tizz and the scores of Charrl which thronged and chirruped about her. She strode angrily up to the Queen of the Hive.

'We had a deal!' she said. 'You said you wouldn't cross over until I tried to bring you some help!'

Ch'tizz turned away from Ace's accusing stare. 'The Charrl must survive,' she said fiercely. 'A broken promise is nothing when compared to the continuance of the Species.'

Ace turned savagely on Muldwych. 'And you said they were the noblest species going!' she reminded him, but she could see that even Muldwych was disturbed by Ch'tizz's reneging on her promise.

'But you can't take over the Earth,' protested Benny. 'What about mankind?'

'The planet is too small: it will not support our two species. The Mammals will have to be destroyed,' Ch'tizz stated coldly. 'Killing goes against the Way of the Charrl; but our Species must survive.'

In the shadows Bellingham grew pale: this talk of destruction was not what he and the other members of the New Dawn had planned. Even Muldwych himself looked shocked.

'When I agreed to help you, you made no mention of killing,' he said.

'Would you have helped me if I had, Muldwych? asked Ch'tizz. 'We have both used each other. We now have a new planet on which to swarm.' She glanced over at the TARDIS. 'And you have what you want, you have your freedom.'

Ace glared evilly at the fat old man: it was all his fault, she realized. If the Charrl destroyed mankind it was Muldwych, in his desperate attempt to escape Antýkhon, who would be to blame.

'You're all out of your tree, Ch'tizz,' Ace said. 'Look at this place. Mankind's already started to screw up the atmosphere, and pollute his own planet . . . '

'Compared to Antýkhon this place is a garden,' said Ch'tizz. 'You at least should realize that.'

'But you can't hope to subjugate the Earth,' countered Benny. 'Earthmen will put up too much resistance. We're barbaric, intolerant, savage. Just look at Ace!'

Thank you very much, Ace thought.

'In only five years' time we'll start a war that will kill nearly ten million,' Benny revealed.

'Then that just proves the innate superiority of the Charrl,' said Ch'tizz. 'A species that kills its own kind has lost all moral right to survive. The Charrl do not kill the Charrl . . . '

Muldwych stepped forward; there was a very worried look on his face now. 'Your Majesty, there are great tracts of this planet where the humans cannot survive: the deserts and polar icecaps, for instance. Surely some arrangement can be made between yourself and the humans . . . '

Ch'tizz paused and thought about the matter.

'Do not go further against the Laws of the Goddess,' Muldwych continued. 'Don't let five thousand years of greatness and nobility be dashed away because of your instinctive desire to survive at whatever the cost. Negotiate with the humans . . . '

Ace and Benny watched on fascinated as Ch'tizz considered the possibility.

'You'll never get mankind to co-operate with a bunch of giant grasshoppers!' Benny whispered.

'I know,' said Ace. 'But let her think we can . . . '

Ch'tizz looked down at Muldwych. 'The humans will talk to us?'

Muldwych nodded, and hoped he sounded convincing. 'I'm sure they will. Let there be no more killing, Ch'tizz . . . '

'We have no wish to kill,' Ch'tizz insisted, but added: 'But the Charrl must survive . . . '

'And so it shall!' said Muldwych. 'Side by side with humanity!'

'Good Lord, I think she's going to buy it!' Benny marvelled.

Ch'tizz was about to speak, when the air exploded with the sound of gunfire. With an angry snarl Ch'tizz turned around. Popov had arrived, together with Korin and Seeba, and an armed detachment of police.

'Miss Benny, get down!' he screamed, and fired on the surprised Charrl.

Oh great! Benny groaned inwardly. *What a time to use your credentials to persuade the police that we're on their side. Perfect timing again, Misha!*

'You still think we should talk to these humans?' asked Ch'tizz as the first of her Charrl was blasted down by Korin's gun. With a blood-chilling screech the Charrl turned on their attackers, and leapt into the fray.

What the police – only twenty of them, together with Popov, Seeba and Korin – lacked in numbers they more than made up for in fire-power. And the Charrl, still shaken by their trip across the Great Divide were clumsy, and their innate respect for all forms of life stayed their hands. Until, that was, the police began to mow them down. Then they realized that they were fighting for their lives, and showed no mercy. With swipes of their deadly claws they sliced at their human attackers until the street was awash with hot, steaming blood, and the anguished cries of dismembered Mammals.

Muldwych looked on horrified as the slaughter increased on both sides; this hadn't been part of his plan.

Ace grabbed him by the shoulders and shook him hard. 'You still think you're in control, do you!'

Muldwych shook his head. 'This isn't supposed to happen,' he said.

'Well, it bloody well is,' cried Benny above the sound of the gunfire and the screeching of the Charrl. 'You got us into this mess: you get us out!'

Muldwych looked at the battle between the police and the Charrl, and then back at the TARDIS.

'Into the TARDIS!' he commanded, suddenly coming to a decision, and bustled Benny and Ace into the police box. 'There's one chance!'

Muldwych strode into the console room – with a disconcerting familiarity, Ace thought. He began flicking a series of controls on one of the instrument panels.

'What are you doing?' asked Ace.

'Gaining a bargaining tool,' he said. 'The TARDIS opened and stabilized the Great Divide. With a bit of luck I can also make her close it – at least for a little while.'

'Why are you so familiar with the TARDIS?' asked Benny, as Muldwych's hands flipped over the controls.

'The Doctor's not the only one with a TARDIS, you know,' he said without looking up. 'I had one too – once . . . '

Benny looked over to Ace as if to ask: *He's a Time Lord?*

Ace shrugged her shoulders: *Don't ask me!*

Muldwych stood back from the control console and clapped his hands in satisfaction.

'There! That's done it!' He stalked out of the open doors back into the East End.

The slaughter was stomach-turning. Police lay dead on the

ground, their guts ripped out and their blood seeping out between the cobblestones. By their side lay shattered and collapsed Charrl, their time-weathered exoskeletons quickly turning into dust.

Benny noticed with satisfaction that Bellingham was one of the dead, struck by (she hoped) a wayward bullet from Popov's revolver.

'Ch'tizz!' cried Muldwych. 'Hear me out!'

Ch'tizz turned, struck by the new authority in the Mammal's voice.

'I have closed the Great Divide. If this killing does not stop, no more of your people will be able to come over.'

Ch'tizz urged her people to halt their attack. Muldwych was about to continue when he felt the icy touch of a blaster on his neck. Seeba had crept up behind him.

'You will open up the Divide again, old man,' he growled. 'You will let the Charrl through.'

'Seeba, are you mad?' asked Ace. 'We're trying to save your planet!'

'Not my planet, Ace. My planet's in the future, remember? And I want the Charrl off it!'

Seeba felt something strike him in the back, as the forgotten Charlie launched into him head first. Ace wrenched the gun off Seeba.

'I have never betrayed your race before, Ch'tizz,' said Muldwych. 'And I don't intend to now.'

'What are you proposing, Muldwych?'

'I can use the TARDIS to shift the location of the Great Divide,' he claimed. 'The Great Divide can take you to another world, an alternative Earth, where mankind never developed.

'A new and innocent world, Ch'tizz, verdant and fresh for colonization; a world where the Charrl need not kill to survive!'

An enormous chirruping came from the Charrl as they considered the situation.

Benny whispered to Muldwych: 'Can you really do that? Send them to an alternative Earth?'

'Of course not.'

Finally Ch'tizz returned to Muldwych. 'We agree. Send us to another Earth, and there will be no more killing . . .'

Chapter 29

Long hours later a weary Muldwych flicked a switch on the TARDIS control console. He sighed with relief. 'That's done it. Seeba and Korin are returned to Antýkhon, the Charrl have their new world, and the Great Divide is closed forever. There'll be nobody else interfering with time.'

'What have you done with the Charrl, Muldwych?' demanded Benny. 'You said that you couldn't send them to another Earth.'

'Oh, I didn't do anything,' he said. 'It was the TARDIS who did all the work . . . '

'The TARDIS? What do you mean?'

'The TARDIS is a craft that transcends all time and space, Ace,' said Muldwych. 'Remember how it shifts and changes, and continually alters its interior dimensions.' He turned to Benny.

'You told me that you entered the TARDIS's "mind". But that is just one of the many dimensions contained within the TARDIS itself. And that's where I've – the TARDIS – *we've* sent them.'

'They're *inside* the TARDIS?' asked Benny in disbelief.

'You could put it like that, yes. They'll be happy there . . . '

'Oh fantastic!' said Ace. 'Not only do we have a swimming pool, and a tennis court, and a cinema, now we've got a bloody insect house on board the TARDIS!'

Muldwych smiled. 'I'm sure I'll be able to drop them off somewhere.'

'But what about all those women who the Charrl have infected?' asked Benny. 'What happens to them?'

'Ah . . . ' said Muldwych. 'Well, when I relocated the Great Divide I made sure that I swept it over London. Like a giant vacuum cleaner, you could say. It was able to pick up the Charrl seed from the women who were infected and transport them along with the rest of their race . . . And Ch'tizz has told me that only five women were infected. I wouldn't worry about it if I were you . . . '

And if you believe that . . . Muldwych thought guiltily.

Muldwych began to operate the TARDIS controls. The great double doors slammed shut. He was about to press his hand down on the main dematerialization lever when Ace stopped him.

'Wait a minute. What do you think you're doing?'

'Taking off,' he replied. 'What do you think I'm doing?'

'We don't go anywhere without the Doctor!' insisted Ace.

'The Doctor!' laughed Muldwych. 'Don't you realize he's left you, abandoned you! He doesn't care in the slightest about you!'

'Maybe so, but he wouldn't abandon the TARDIS without good reason.'

Muldwych sulked, but there was a sly look in his eyes.

'Wouldn't he? He has no use for the TARDIS now. But for me it means my survival – my freedom from an eternal exile on Antýkhon! It's my right: I saved the Earth from the Charrl!'

'You were the one who brought them there in the first place,' Benny pointed out. 'If not for you those women, Margaret Waterfield, wouldn't have died . . . '

'Just who are you, Muldwych?' demanded Ace. 'A Time Lord?'

'Aha,' said Muldwych mysteriously and brought his hand once more down on the main dematerialization control. Benny tried to drag his hand away but with an angry snarl the old man pushed her away and drove the final lever home.

'I must have my freedom!' he cried, as the time rotor began its steady rise and fall, and the TARDIS vanished from Edwardian England.

'And no one should stand in my way.'

Suddenly the time rotor lurched to a halt, and the entire control chamber shook. Muldwych looked wild-eyed at the two women. 'What have you done?' he demanded.

'Not us,' said Benny. Was it her imagination, or could she hear from somewhere far off the bleating of a Lamb – or was it the howl of a Wolf? 'It's the TARDIS . . . she doesn't want you here!'

Muldwych looked all about him. 'No! You can't!' he cried out to the time machine. 'You can't confine me to exile on one insignificant planet in a narrow intergalactic backwater! I *belong* here!'

His eyes rapidly scanned the display panels in the console, desperately searching for some means to halt the TARDIS's actions. But the TARDIS had taken control now, and would no longer tolerate Muldwych interfering in her plans.

Muldwych activated one control after another, all to no avail. The time rotor resumed its rise and fall, and the control chamber was filled with the familiar sound of dematerialization.

'Look at Muldwych!' said Benny.

Muldwych raised his hands to his head in horror, trying to shut out the noise. Slowly he began to fade away, until all that remained of him was his shrieks of horror and disappointment. The TARDIS had expelled him from her system –

– and sent him fifteen thousand years into the future, to a barren world called Antýkhon, there to await its colonization by a noble race of insects called the Charrl.

'Wicked . . . ' whistled Ace.

Benny looked around the control chamber. 'I never realized the TARDIS had that sort of power . . . '

'The Doctor always referred to it as "she",' remarked Ace. 'I guess we now know why . . . '

She wandered over to the control console. 'So what do we do now, Benny? No Doctor . . . '

'We've got the TARDIS, I suppose,' said Benny.

The door leading to the interior of the TARDIS clicked open and there stood the last person they ever expected to see again.

'Doctor!'

'Professor, where the hell have you been?'

The Doctor affected an air of detached amusement. 'Been? Why, nowhere of course. I've been in my quarters all this time.'

His nose and cheeks were red. He brushed something from his shoulder. Flakes of melting ice. *In your quarters,* thought Ace. *Pull the other one.*

Benny looked at the Doctor in bitter disbelief. 'People have died while you've been "in your quarters",' she said, and added as an afterthought, 'The flowers were a nice thought, by the way . . . '

'Flowers?' The Doctor looked guilty, and began to inspect the TARDIS control panels.

'Margaret Waterfield,' Benny said. 'It was a very quiet funeral . . . '

'Ah . . . '

'Just what exactly are you up to, Doctor?' asked Benny.

By her side, Ace remained silent; she'd known the Doctor too long to bother asking any more.

The Doctor turned back to Benny. 'You seem to have got by quite well without me,' he said.

'That's not the point.'

'Isn't it?' he asked her, and fixed her with those piercing eyes of his. 'Remember what you were like before you met me, Ace? Or you, Benny? Could you have got by so well without me then?'

As a matter of fact, yes, Benny thought.

The Doctor turned his attention back to the central control console, and began adjusting the controls. 'I can't be here with you forever, you know. Remember: I'm not human. There are other places to visit, others' problems to sort out. Keep that in mind, Benny. Doctors are supposed to mend things, to heal the infected, guide the confused. If I were just another man in the street you might as well call me John Smith . . . '

'But . . . ' said Benny.

The Doctor turned around and placed a silencing finger on her lips.

'Them that ask no questions . . . '

Benny glared at him. 'I know – "don't get told no lies".'

First Epilogue:

Earth, January AD 1910

'Congratulations, m'lady, it's a boy! And a bonnier specimen I've never seen.'

The midwife's voice was strained, and it was plain that she didn't mean it. But nevertheless Francesca Whitton loved her child; and even though it had been the result of that terrible experience she had had in London's East End nine months ago, when she had been trying to improve the lot of the working girls of Whitechapel, still she vowed that she would love it with all her heart.

She took hold of her baby and turned it towards her. Its bright bulbous eyes shone with a brilliant intensity, and its long gangly limbs reached out lovingly to its human mother. Here was a child that would go far in the world! Here was a child that its mother loved with all her heart.

Aye, and it's a face that only a mother would love! thought the Scottish midwife. She frowned and sniffed the air: there was a faint whiff of ammonia. She'd better find the cause of it. Otherwise it might be harmful to the mother and her newborn child . . .

Second Epilogue:

The planet Antýkhon

The Doctor sipped at his tea: it was too sweet for his liking, and the whisky in it made him grimace. Still, it would be bad manners to insult his host.

'You've caused a lot of bad feeling, Muldwych,' he said to the fat little man. 'Your cold-hearted manipulation to win your freedom has caused a lot of deaths . . . '

'*My* manipulation, Doctor?' said Muldwych. 'You are a fine one to talk! Because of my interference Jared Khan has been defeated. He'd been on your trail for seven hundred years, you know.'

The Doctor smiled. 'I knew . . . '

'And the Charrl have been given a new life,' Muldwych continued. 'And with the Charrl off Antýkhon the Earth is now free to be recolonized by humanity . . . Not bad for a cold-hearted manipulator, I'd say.'

'You're still trapped, exiled on Antýkhon – without any means of escape . . . '

'You could help me . . . '

The Doctor smiled and shook his head. 'Against all the Laws of Time, I'm afraid. I shouldn't even be here sitting talking to you now, you know. You got yourself into this little mess, and it's up to you to get yourself out of it. I never meddle in other people's lives – unless it's absolutely unavoidable.'

'It usually is, though, isn't it?'

The Doctor stood up wearily and walked over to the window where he looked down on the vast plain below: dead and barren now, but there was once a time when it had been a lush wilderness supporting uncountable numbers of different species.

'I was here a long time ago, you know,' he mused. 'Down there on the plain. It was there that I saw a hunter shoot dead the last lion on Earth . . . '

'I know,' said Muldwych, 'I remember . . . '

'Sad, very sad,' said the Doctor and shook his head. He looked back up at Muldwych. 'Ace wanted to know who you were, you know.'

'You told her?'

'No. It will remain our little secret. But I think she guesses . . . '

'Clever girl,' said Muldwych. 'Did you give her my present?'

'*Madame Bovary*?' asked the Doctor. 'Yes, but she's much more interested in her back copies of *Soldier of Fortune* magazine. I fear she's not too taken with nineteenth-century French literature.'

'She'll have to be one day.'

'I know.' The Doctor stood up to go. 'Muldwych, I have to leave. I've outstayed my time here as it is.'

'You always do, Doctor,' he said and showed him to the door. 'When will you return? It gets lonely in my exile here. Your tales are the only thing I look forward to, you know.'

'I'll be here from time to time,' said the Doctor. 'And in the meantime, do try and stay out of the affairs of the Hairies down there on Antýkhon. We're not supposed to interfere, you know. D'you think you'll be able to do that, Muldwych?'

The fat little man sniggered. 'Who knows, Doctor? Who knows?'

With a knowing grin the Doctor made his way down Mount Kukūruk and back to the waiting TARDIS.